THE ICE CHILDREN

THE ICE CHILDREN

M. G. LEONARD

ILLUSTRATED BY PENNY NEVILLE-LEE

MACMILLAN CHILDREN'S BOOKS

First published as an original audiobook by Audible

This edition published 2023 by Macmillan Children's Books
an imprint of Pan Macmillan
The Smithson, 6 Briset Street, London EC1M 5NR
EU representative: Macmillan Publishers Ireland Ltd, 1st Floor,
The Liffey Trust Centre, 117–126 Sheriff Street Upper
Dublin 1, D01 YC43
Associated companies throughout the world
www.panmacmillan.com

ISBN 978-1-0350-1421-7

1 3 5 7 9 8 6 4 2

A CIP catalogue record for this book is available from the British Library.

Printed and bound by CPI Group (UK) Ltd, Croydon CR0 4YY

For Kirsty, my guardian angel

1

THE ICE BOY

O nce upon a warm winter, in the dawning darkness of December, a boy was found in the city rose garden. He was dressed in navy starred pyjamas. The pale skin of his face was duck-egg blue and sparkled with snow crystals. Every strand of his fine blond hair was an ashen icicle. His eyes were closed, his expression serene. His feet were submerged in a pedestal of ice.

The boy looked like a statue. He was frozen solid.

'How is this possible?' said the police officer, gazing with horror at the lifeless figure and thinking of her own children, tucked up in their beds. 'Sarge says a five-year-old boy matching his description was reported missing half an hour ago. His name is Finn Albedo.'

Without taking her eyes off the child's face, she removed her hat and nervously ran her fingers through her hair. 'Doctor, his parents are on their way here, now. What am I going to tell them?'

'The truth.' The doctor was wrapped in the thick woollen coat that accompanied him on late-night calls. He stepped back from the frozen boy. 'You can tell them that he is alive. I can hear his heartbeat through my stethoscope. It's very slow, but he *is* alive.' He shook his head, and his melancholy voice took on a note of wonder. 'Never in all my years have I seen anything like this.'

The sound of footsteps made them both turn.

Mr and Mrs Albedo ran into the rose garden, clutching the hand of a solemn-faced eleven-year-old girl with fierce hazel eyes and bobbed brown hair. She was wearing a winter coat over her nightie and wellington boots with no socks.

The sight of her brother hit Bianca hard, snatching the breath from her body. He was so still, so blue. Framed by twinkling stars and spotlit by the full moon's beam, he looked unsettlingly beautiful. She dropped her mother's hand.

'Is he dead?' Bianca whispered, terror rising inside her.

'Now, you mustn't panic,' said the doctor.

But Bianca was remembering the fight she'd had with Finn at bedtime. He wouldn't let her see the book he'd borrowed from the library and she'd got cross, calling him the most annoying little brother in the whole world. Finn had cried and she'd lost her temper, saying he was behaving like a baby and that she wished she had a little sister instead. Now, her cruel words and his tears echoed in her head. Had he run away because of her?

'Who did this?' Bianca's dad asked angrily. 'Tell me who did this to my son, right now!'

'We don't know, sir.' The officer took out her notepad. 'All we know is that a person named Jack Dewynter was taking a night-time stroll through the park and found your son . . . like this.' She gestured.

3

'He reported it to one of the constables on night duty.'

'We put him to bed, like normal, with a book . . .' Bianca's mum's voice was high and wavering as she reached out and touched Finn's icy arm. 'But I found his bedroom door open. His bed empty!' She pressed her lips together, trying not to cry, and tucked a wisp of her auburn hair behind her ear. 'He's only five.'

'How did Finn get here? Like this . . . here, in the park?' her dad asked the police officer, struggling to make sense of what had happened. He was a practical man, a problem solver, but you couldn't solve a problem if you didn't know what it was. And for the first time Bianca saw that he had wrinkles across his forehead and looked old.

'We don't know, sir. Nothing like this has ever happened before. It's very . . . strange.' The officer shrugged apologetically. 'The doctor says his heart is still beating.'

'He's alive?' Bianca's dad's voice rang with a tremulous note of hope, and they all turned to the doctor.

'Hem . . . well, yes,' the doctor said, sounding cautious. 'He has a heartbeat.'

'Then we must free him!' Bianca's dad slid off his coat, passing it to her mum, signalling that she should put it on Finn. 'Should we warm him up?'

4

'Ah . . . er . . . well, in severe cases of frostbite one must be on the lookout for muscle and bone damage. Although this doesn't look like frostbite to me. Er . . .' The doctor stroked his chin. 'It is a most unusual case. Until we know what has actually caused this, I really don't think it's a good idea to try and move your son. We don't want to . . . accidentally hurt him.'

'Frozen things can shatter,' the police officer said, and Bianca's mum gasped with horror.

'What's wrong with you?' her dad snapped at the police officer, putting his arm round her mum, whose head had bowed and shoulders slumped.

'I apologize. That was thoughtless of me. What I meant was—'

'I know what you meant,' Bianca's mother sobbed.

Stepping away from her parents, Bianca reached out, taking her brother's icy hand. He was as cold as stone. The

pedestal raised him half a metre, so he was taller than her. She looked up at his face, and her thoughts jumped back a week, to when she had chased him up the stairs after his bath, pretending to be a hungry monster trying to eat him. How warm and pink he'd been when they'd tumbled onto his bedroom carpet together, laughing.

'I don't really want a sister, Finn,' she whispered, her heart aching. 'I was being mean when I said that. I'm sorry. I really am. You're not a baby. You're the best brother in the world.'

Silence.

'What should we do?' her dad asked, sounding desperate and helpless. 'Tell us. Please.'

'This is an unprecedented situation.' The officer was shaking her head. 'There was a girl who fell through the ice into the boating lake three years ago, but this . . . this is different.'

'Somebody did it to him,' Bianca said, and the adults turned their heads. The police officer blinked, looking surprised, as if she'd forgotten Bianca was there. 'Finn didn't freeze himself. Somebody froze him!' She scanned the rose garden. It looked different at night. Less friendly. 'Why aren't you searching for clues?'

Bianca saw several curious bystanders peering at

her brother through a gap in the hedgerow. A couple, leaning into each other, looked as if they were on their way home from a night out. Behind them stood a towering man in a long black coat, dark glasses and a top hat. He was watching her. She scowled at him, then turned her angry eyes to the officer. 'You should be interviewing people, looking for clues and detecting things! What's happened to Finn is a crime. What did that Mr Dewynter man say? Did you arrest him?'

'Neither taking a walk nor reporting something is a crime.' The police officer shook her head.

It dawned on Bianca that Finn being frozen might not be a crime either. Could something be a crime if it had never happened before?

'Don't you worry about your little brother.' The police officer's mouth curved into a fake smile. Bianca recognized it as one that grown-ups used when they wanted children to stop asking awkward questions. 'We're doing everything we can for him.'

Bianca glared at her. If the police weren't going to investigate properly, then she would do it herself.

Kneeling down, she moved carefully around the pedestal of ice, studying it. It was transparent, and with the help of the full moon, she could see crushed grass through the base.

'Well, the ice didn't spring out of the ground and

catch you like a Venus flytrap,' Bianca muttered to Finn. 'If it had, there'd be no grass underneath it.'

Scattered around the base of the pedestal were large hailstones. Bianca picked one up, rolling it between her thumb and forefinger. For weeks the weather had been wet and warm. There hadn't even been a frost yet. Where had the hailstones and ice come from?

Ignoring the burning cold, Bianca ran her hands over the pedestal's surface. The back and the sides were smooth, but the front had indentations. Her fingers explored them. 'Words!' she gasped, bringing her nose closer to the ice.

In carved italic capital letters, she read:

DARK DAYS GROW EVER WARMER.
WINTER'S ON THE RUN.
ICE BECOMES A LIQUID,
BENEATH A SEARING SUN.
WHEN THE SEASONS ALTER,
SOMETHING MUST BE DONE.
WITH THE HEARTS OF CHILDREN,
WINTER WILL LIVE ON.

'Mum! Dad! Look!' Bianca cried. 'There's writing here! What do you think it means?'

Her parents, the officer and the doctor all crowded

around to see, reading the words with expressions of disbelief and revulsion.

'Is this someone's idea of a sick joke?' Her dad almost choked as he spoke, he was so angry.

The police officer and doctor shook their heads, not daring to reply.

The poem made no sense to Bianca, but she felt it must be a clue. 'I'm going to find out who did this to you, Finn,' she whispered, looking up at her brother. 'I promise. I *will* save you.'

2

A VANISHING BOOK

When Bianca woke up, she found she was lying on top of her duvet, on her bed, still wearing her coat and wellington boots. Her first thought was of Finn. She hoped wildly that last night had been a bad dream, but her clothing told her it hadn't been. Her heart felt heavy. A storm of tears was brewing behind her eyes. Poor Finn, all alone in the park. Was he cold? Was he frightened?

'Being sad won't help him,' she scolded herself. She had seen how it had disarmed her dad, who usually had a plan for every situation, and her mum couldn't stop crying once she had started. Bianca decided she would be brave and strong for her brother.

Shivering as she got up, she breathed out a white

mist. Her bedroom was freezing. Why hadn't the heating come on?

Three of the walls in Bianca's bedroom were painted lilac-grey but the fourth wall was her favourite. It was papered with a blue-and-white winter woodland scene. Reindeer peeped round trees, foxes were curled up in underground dens, and squirrels perched on snowy branches, clutching acorns. She faced the woodland, doing star jumps until she felt warmth returning to her numb limbs. Running on the spot as fast as she could, she chanted under her breath, 'Wake up, wake up, *wake up!*'

She needed to switch on her brain. She'd made a promise to free Finn from the ice and find the person responsible. She intended to keep it.

Perhaps, if it's sunny today, the ice around Finn will melt, she thought, going to the window and whipping the curtain aside.

The view startled her.

Yesterday it had been warm enough for her not to need a jumper under her coat. Today thick impenetrable clouds hovered over the city rooftops like a flock of sullen sheep waiting to be shorn of their snowy fleeces.

On the outside of the window, frost fractals had created patterns that looked like tiny ferns and ostrich-feather fans.

Bianca pulled her coat around her and wondered if this was what the grown-ups called a 'cold snap'. It hadn't been like this yesterday.

Today was Saturday. No school meant she had the whole day to investigate. She would start right away. Throwing open her wardrobe, she pulled out her

warmest clothes, putting on thermal underwear, thick leggings and two pairs of socks. A thought made her open her bottom drawer. Inside was a jumper she'd never worn. Her mother had knitted it for her as a Christmas gift. One arm was longer than the other, the neck gaped, and it hung down almost to her knees. The wool was a soft warm purple and it had a white *B* on the front, for Bianca. She'd tried to hide her disappointment when she'd opened it last Christmas. Her mum had declared that she looked wonderful in it, but Bianca had hidden it in her bottom drawer and not looked at it since. It might cheer Mum up to see her wearing it today. She put it on over her thermal vest and looked at herself in the mirror, nodding. This felt like the right uniform for a mission to save Finn.

Pulling her coat back on, Bianca went to her desk, picking up her pocket-sized orange diary and a pen. She would need a notebook, to write things down, like the police officer had last night.

She marched along the landing. The low rumble of adult voices drifted up the stairs and she wondered if her parents had gone to bed at all last night. She didn't think they had.

The first thing to do was to inspect the scene of the crime. Something had happened last night in her brother's bedroom that had led to him leaving the house and ending up in the park, frozen on a pedestal of ice.

She opened her brother's bedroom door. A higgledy-piggledy fantasy land sprawled across Finn's carpet. Toy train tracks wove around exotic animals, a pirate ship, a teddy bears' picnic, a giant plastic Tyrannosaurus rex and buildings constructed from brightly coloured blocks. Bianca tiptoed across the floor, not wanting to disturb anything. She studied the room in sections, hunting for anything out of place or out of the ordinary. She checked the window. It was closed, locked and patterned with frost. There were no signs of it having been opened.

Finn's bedding was ruckled, and Bianca's heart twisted as her eyes landed on his favourite cuddly toy. Sposh, a white rabbit wearing a cheerful red scarf, lay abandoned on Finn's pillow. She picked up the bunny and hugged it. Finn had been three when they'd first visited the city zoo together. He'd fallen in love with the bunny in the gift shop. He'd taken it from the shelf, chattering away to it as if it had been sitting there waiting for him. Her parents had had no choice but to buy it. Finn and Sposh had been inseparable ever since. Except now Sposh was here, and Finn was in the ice. If Finn had left the house of his own will, in the dark, Bianca knew he would have taken Sposh with him.

Perching on the edge of her brother's bed, cuddling his bunny, Bianca carefully went through the events of the previous day. It had been a Friday. They'd gone to school, like normal. Dad had picked them up and taken them to the library, like normal. They'd come home and eaten dinner: fish fingers, chips and peas. Then she'd asked to see Finn's library book. It had a sparkling silver cover and she had wanted to look at it, but he wouldn't let her. They'd fought. Mum, exasperated by their bickering, had sent them to their separate bedrooms. And then they'd gone to bed, like normal. But something desperately abnormal had to have happened for Finn to leave the house in the night.

'*There's something I'm not seeing!*' she said to herself.

A mournful voice inside her head told her that the thing she wasn't seeing was her little brother, sitting cross-legged on his bedroom floor, playing happily

15

with his toys, as he always did on a Saturday morning.

There was a pile of books on the floor in front of the bedside table, and Bianca thought she might look at Finn's library book. The one he hadn't let her see yesterday. She leaned her hand on the pile, to bend down, and found that the top book was wet, as if a glass of water had been spilt on it. She wiped her hand on the bedcovers, and read the stack of spines. None of them sparkled like his library book had. Thinking that Finn might have been reading it when he fell asleep, Bianca checked down the gap where the bed frame butted up against the wall, then underneath the bed. No book. Picking her way across the toy-strewn floor, she looked in Finn's bookcase, but it wasn't there either.

'It must be here somewhere,' Bianca muttered to herself, puzzled. Eventually she gave up, assuming the book must be in Mum and Dad's room, or downstairs. She pushed it to the back of her mind. She was determined to complete her mission and conduct a thorough search of the house for clues.

3

THE LIBRARY

Bianca pushed the kitchen door open and found her father standing at the cooker dressed in the same navy trousers and fisherman's jumper he had been wearing last night. His shoulders were hunched, as if he were wearing an invisible rucksack filled with stones.

'Where's Mum?' Bianca asked.

'In the rose garden with Finn.' Dad's voice was scratchy. He sounded tired. 'I'm making porridge,' he said, without turning around. 'Do you want some? I'm taking the pot to the park. Your mum thinks we should try and give it to Finn, though I don't see how.' He stopped stirring and stared straight ahead.

Bianca came to stand beside her father's elbow. She

wasn't hungry. The thought of eating made her feel nauseous, but she knew she would need energy today. She watched him pour the steaming gloopy oats into a bowl and add a dollop of raspberry jam.

'Dad, have you seen Finn's book anywhere? The one he brought home from the library yesterday?'

'Finn's book?' He added a splash of milk and passed her the bowl.

'Yes.' She sat down at the table. 'I've looked everywhere, but I can't find it.'

'Can't find what?' her dad said, distracted.

'Finn's silver book! The one he got from the library.'

'If it's lost, I'll pay for it.'

Bianca was about to explain that she wasn't worried about a fine, but she saw the faraway look in her father's eyes and fell silent.

He put the lid on the saucepan, wrapped it in a hand towel and eased it into a cloth bag. 'Eat up your breakfast. When you're done, we'll go to the park to join your mum and Finn.'

As she shovelled the hot porridge into her mouth, Bianca couldn't help thinking about the missing book. She'd been through the whole house. Everything seemed as it always was; the only odd thing was her not being able to find that book. It bothered her. Why couldn't she find it? Was it a clue? Perhaps Mum had read the book to Finn at bedtime? She should ask her about it, but Bianca was afraid of bothering her mother with questions about what had happened last night. She didn't want to upset her. She wished she knew the name of the story, or at least the author, then she could find out what the mysterious book was about.

'Are you ready, Bianca?' her dad called from the front door.

'Yes,' Bianca called back, jumping up and spooning down the last few mouthfuls of breakfast.

Stepping outside, Bianca was shocked by the drop in temperature. She gasped as an icy wind slapped her cheeks. 'Do you think it will snow?' she said, looking up at the low clouds.

'Possibly,' her dad grunted.

Normally, after spotting the first tiny drifting flake, her dad would dive into the garden shed and drag out the sledges. He loved the snow. But today he was closed off from the world, and from her. On the way to the park, she had to jog to keep up with his hurried strides. The people they passed were wrapped in coats, thick scarves and woolly hats. Some paused and stared.

'Why are people looking at us?' Bianca whispered. 'I don't like it.'

'They must have heard about Finn.'

She slipped her hand into his and they walked on together.

Opposite the entrance to the park was the grand circular stone building that held the city library. Seeing it gave Bianca an idea. She stopped, pulling at her dad's hand so that he halted too. 'Please may I go to the library? I know how to use the pelican crossing safely and I'll come and find you and Mum as soon as I'm done.'

Her dad looked puzzled by the request. 'OK, but don't go getting yourself into any trouble.'

'I won't. I promise.'

'And come straight to the rose garden when you're done. Do you hear me?'

'I will.'

She felt him watching her as she ran up the stone steps, past the columns that propped up the vestibule roof and in through the giant wooden doors.

Bianca headed straight for the children's section at the back of the ground floor. The librarian's desk was situated beneath a colourful mural of teddy bears at a picnic. To the right of the desk was a semicircle of giant red cushions arranged around a blue circular rug. On them children sat reading – the younger ones snuggled on parents' laps.

'Bianca!' Mrs Dorcas, the kindly librarian, looked surprised to see her. Bianca noticed one or two of the parents shooting furtive glances her way and wrapping their arms around their babies. 'Can I help you?'

Bianca could see from the look on Mrs Dorcas's face that she knew about Finn. A bubble of sadness grew inside her chest as she saw pity in the librarian's eyes. She knew if the bubble popped she'd cry. She couldn't let herself get upset. She needed to think straight. She cleared her throat.

'Yes, please, Mrs Dorcas. My brother, Finn, took a book out yesterday, after school. It's silver, sparkly and about this big . . .' She grabbed a picture book from the returns trolley to show her. 'I need to know what it was called and who it was by. Could you help me find out?'

'I'm sure I can.' Mrs Dorcas blinked and looked down at her computer, typing something in and clicking her mouse. 'It's just a matter of looking up your brother's name on the system.' Mrs Dorcas frowned as she scanned the computer screen. 'You say Finn took a book out yesterday?'

'Yes. We both did.'

'I can see that *you* did, Bianca dear, but your brother hasn't taken out a book since last Friday, although he did return one yesterday.'

'But he *did*!' Bianca exclaimed in surprise. 'He brought it home. He wouldn't let me read it.'

'According to the computer, he didn't.'

'Could the computer be wrong?' Bianca didn't know what to think. She remembered seeing Finn leaving the library with the silver book under his arm. If he hadn't got it from here, then where had he got it from?

'It isn't usually wrong,' Mrs Dorcas said softly, seeing the distress on Bianca's face. 'Would it help if I found you another copy? Oh, but you said you don't know what it's called or who it's by? Do you know what it's about?'

Bianca shook her head, and the bubble inside her chest grew.

'Oh dear. I'm afraid that does make things difficult. I can't recall a single sparkly book that matches your description.' She pointed to a free-standing set of shelves. 'If there is one, it might be over there.'

Bianca thanked the librarian and went to the bookcase. If she had to, she would check every single book in the library. Her skin prickled; she had a feeling that the missing book was important in some way.

After an hour, Bianca had systematically gone through every shelf in the children's library and found nothing that resembled the silver book. Noticing the time, she realized she would have to give up and come back another day to continue her search in the rest of the library. Her parents would be wondering where she'd got to. She would have to be brave and ask her mum if she knew what had happened to Finn's book.

On her way to the door, someone rushed past Bianca, bumping her shoulder. It was a girl she recognized from school called Sophie Lilley. She was hurrying out of the library, and under her arm she clutched a silver book just like Finn's.

4

SOPHIE LILLEY

'**S**ophie! Wait!' Bianca called out, and was immediately *shushed* by other people in the library. She sprinted to catch up with the girl, keeping her eyes glued firmly on the silver book.

'Hi, Bianca,' Sophie said as they passed through the library doors together and came out onto the stone steps.

Sophie was an athletic girl with long honey-coloured hair and a cheeky grin. She wasn't in the same class as Bianca, but they were both in the school netball team. Sophie was the captain and played centre. She was a natural leader, outgoing and kind.

'Where did you get that book?' Bianca asked, her hand reaching towards it.

'The library,' Sophie replied. 'Why?'

'I've been looking for it all morning,' Bianca said. 'Can I see it?'

'No.' Sophie stepped away from Bianca, moving the book so it was behind her back.

'I only want to look at it.'

'This is *my* book.' Sophie narrowed her eyes, and Bianca was startled by her cold expression. Sophie was usually so generous and friendly.

Bianca took a step back. 'I just want to know the name of the book and who it's by. My brother brought it home yesterday—'

'Go away!' Sophie shouted, pivoting, clutching the book to her chest. 'It's mine. You can't have it.' And she ran, jumping down the last two steps, and sprinted away.

Bianca was shocked. She had never seen Sophie

behave like this. She thought about running after her, but Sophie was fast. And what would Bianca do if she caught up? Try to take the book from her? Sophie was clearly not going to let it go. Bianca remembered seeing a similar look on Finn's face when she'd asked to see his book last night. That was what had started their fight.

Sitting down on the steps, Bianca took her orange diary from her pocket and wrote down what had happened. How was it that Sophie had found a copy of the book when Bianca had looked everywhere for it? Had she missed a shelf? Where had Sophie found it? And why wouldn't she let her look at it? Bianca was beginning to suspect that this was no ordinary book.

Rising to her feet and crossing the road, Bianca entered the park, taking the route through the rock garden and past the boating lake to the rose garden. Her stomach clenched at the thought of seeing Finn in the light of day. Last night he had seemed peaceful, almost magical, but she feared that, in the daylight, she might see signs of distress.

When she arrived at the entrance to the rose garden, an opening in the hedgerow, she was alarmed to see it was blocked by people. She heard her dad call out her name as she pushed through the crowd. A police officer, a young man, helped her through a barrier of yellow tape that had been put in place to keep back the curious onlookers.

Her mum was standing beside Finn, gently rubbing his frozen arms. She was wearing her sheepskin jacket and a blue bobble hat. Tendrils of her auburn hair coiled down her back like skinny snakes. Bianca was struck once again by how angelic her little brother looked on his pedestal of ice. He glowed with a gentle blue light. It was clear that her parents' attempts to thaw him had failed.

There was a newspaper on the ground beside the park bench where her mum and dad had put their bags. The front-page headline read: *The Ice Child!* Bianca picked it up and scanned the short article. It didn't name Finn, but it reported where he was in the city park. She spotted copies clutched by several people in the crowd and felt a wave of anger. Did they think this was a freak show? Had they all come to gawp at her brother, the ice child?

She felt an arm round her shoulder and looked up into her mum's brown eyes.

'You're wearing the jumper I made you?' Her mum tried to smile.

'I love it,' Bianca replied fiercely.

'Come and sit with me on the bench.'

They sat down together, and Bianca noticed her mum's nose was pink from the cold.

'Are you all right?' her mum asked.

'Are *you* all right?' Bianca replied.

'No,' her mum admitted, chewing her bottom lip.

'Me neither.'

'I wish I knew what to tell you.' Her mother sighed and Bianca saw her eyes fill with tears. 'I don't understand what's happening.'

They looked at Finn for a long moment.

'Mum, can I ask you about Finn's bedtime last night?'

'I've been over it with the police, and with your father.'

'I need to hear what happened.' Bianca swallowed. 'I never got to say goodnight to him. We had that fight, remember? You sent me to my room . . .' She fell silent.

'Oh, Bianca. I'm sorry.' Her mother looked down. 'Let's see. I told Finn to get into his pyjamas and clean his teeth at seven o'clock. When he was done, he said goodnight to Dad, and then I tucked him up in bed. He was hugging Sposh. Then I read him a story, kissed his forehead, turned on his nightlight and turned off the main light.'

'Do you remember which story you read Finn?' Bianca leaned close.

'Erm . . . now let me see.'

'Was it from the silver book he brought back from the library?'

'Do you know . . .' Bianca's mother frowned. 'I'm not sure if I did read to him. I thought I had . . .' Her bottom lip trembled.

'I'm sure you did,' Bianca tried to reassure her.

'But maybe I didn't. I mean, I can't have read him a story if I don't remember the book, can I?'

'The shock has probably made you forget,' Bianca said, feeling the hairs rise on the back of her neck. 'I don't suppose you know where Finn's library book is, do you?'

Her mother shook her head, looking perplexed.

Bianca knew her mum had a good memory. If she lost her gym socks, or Dad lost his keys, Mum always knew where they were. It was odd that she couldn't remember reading to Finn.

Lunch was a round of sandwiches brought to them by the police. Bianca ate hers sitting at Finn's feet, staring up at him, willing him to move.

'Twitch your fingers if you can hear me,' she told him, but Finn didn't move a frozen muscle. She tried everything she could think of to make him respond. She told him he'd left Sposh at home, and that the rabbit missed him. She told him that if he moved they could go home and play Bonky Smash, a raucous game they'd invented when he was three, where they'd bounce on their parents' bed trying to knock each other down onto the mattress. Eventually Bianca fell silent. Nothing worked.

Dinner was a takeaway and, as it grew darker and colder, the gawking crowds silently filtered away.

Bianca's dad suggested they all go home and get some rest, but her mum wouldn't hear of it. 'What if Finn wakes up and I'm not here? He'll be scared,' she pointed out. 'I'm not leaving. You can take Bianca home.'

'But I can't leave you here alone all night.'

'We'll all stay,' Bianca said firmly. 'I don't want to go home without Finn.'

Sleeping bags and a small tent appeared from somewhere. Bianca's dad pitched the tent beside the bench and insisted her mum get into a sleeping bag and try to get some sleep. Mum curled up on the park bench using Dad's lap as her pillow. She said she wouldn't be able to sleep and wanted to watch over Finn.

Bianca climbed into the tent and took out her diary, scribbling down the strange details of her mother's failure to remember Finn's book. She felt frustrated. The book was the only lead she had, and she hadn't learned anything about it. Tomorrow, she would go to Sophie Lilley's house and beg to see it.

As it got late, Bianca's eyes grew heavy. Realizing she could barely keep them open, she wriggled into a sleeping bag and positioned herself so she could see Finn through the tent flaps.

*

The chimes of midnight from the City Hall clock echoed across the park and woke Bianca. For a moment she was confused, but the sight of Finn through the tent door orientated her. She felt a stirring in the air and scrambled out of her sleeping bag. As she emerged from the tent, she fancied she heard the wind chuckling like a naughty child. Her pulse quickened. Something was wrong.

She spotted a woman running along the path beside the rose garden.

'Where are you going?' Bianca called out.

'They've found another child,' the woman replied without stopping. 'Another ice child.'

Bianca gasped, turning to her parents. They were both fast asleep on the bench, her dad slumped down over her mum. She grabbed her sleeping bag and gently covered her father. It was bitingly cold.

'I have to go,' she whispered to their sleeping faces. 'It could help Finn. I won't be long.' And with that she ran, heading in the direction the woman had been going. She saw a gaggle of people around the bandstand and sprinted towards them as fast as she could.

In the middle of the bandstand, standing on a pedestal of ice, was a girl in a nightshirt and shorts, a waterfall of honey hair down her back. Her arms were crossed, her eyes closed and she had a happy grin on her pale frozen face. It was Sophie Lilley.

5

THE MAN IN THE TOP HAT

Bianca heard a keening scream. She didn't need to see the woman to know it had come from Sophie's mother. The harrowing sound was a chord of love, loss and fear. The growing group of onlookers silently parted when the doctor arrived in his thick woollen coat. He opened his bag, put on his stethoscope and pressed it to the frozen girl's chest.

'She is alive,' he pronounced, and Sophie's mother wilted into the arms of a police officer.

Bianca stared at Sophie's happy face. 'Did the silver book do this to you?' she whispered, almost certain that it had.

Like a shoal of fish when the tide turns, the people

either side of her moved and she heard a ripple of murmurs.

'Another child's been frozen!' a man whispered loudly. 'A boy, beside the boating lake.'

This news hit Bianca like lightning. She bolted away, running as fast as she could down to the lake. She was one of the first to reach the boy. He was sitting cross-legged on another pedestal of ice, positioned beside

the water. He looked like a sleeping god, his head turned up towards the full moon, an enigmatic smile on his lips. His eyes were closed and his brown skin was dusted with snow.

'Casper! Oh no!' Bianca gasped, staring at her kind and clever friend, whom she walked to school with, who laughed at her stories and helped her in maths when she struggled. Blinking back tears, she reached out, placing her hand on his chest, and thought she felt the languid throb of his chilled heart. Crouching down, she saw the same words that were carved into her brother's pedestal.

DARK DAYS GROW EVER WARMER.
WINTER'S ON THE RUN.
ICE BECOMES A LIQUID,
BENEATH A SEARING SUN.
WHEN THE SEASONS ALTER,
SOMETHING MUST BE DONE.
WITH THE HEARTS OF CHILDREN,
WINTER WILL LIVE ON.

A police officer laid a gentle hand on Bianca's shoulder, drawing her away from her classmate. 'Where are your parents?'

'Over there,' Bianca replied, pointing in the direction of the rose garden.

'Please return to them.' He had a roll of yellow tape and began to cordon off the area around Casper.

Bianca retreated, her mind reeling. Sophie and Casper! Two more frozen children! A shiver of fear crept up her spine, and suddenly she wanted to be with her family more than anything. She stepped off the path to take a short cut across the grass back to the rose garden, and that was when she noticed the towering form of a man in a long, dark coat, wearing dark glasses and a top hat. He was standing at the edge of the group of concerned onlookers.

Bianca froze.

This man had been looking at Finn last night. The moon lit up one side of his face and his expression chilled her blood. He was smiling. Not a sad smile, but a triumphant one, and the sight of his pointed teeth made her gasp.

Like a crocodile, she thought.

Darting behind a tree, she watched the man. He appeared to be muttering to himself, although she couldn't hear what he was saying. Eventually he turned and walked away. His body moved in the most peculiar way, as if he were made of spaghetti.

Without thinking about whether it was dangerous, Bianca followed him.

As the news that more children had been found frozen spread through the city, concerned and curious folk trickled into the park. The tall man walked with his spaghetti strides against the flow of newcomers. He was easy to follow. Bianca kept her eyes fixed on his top hat.

Heading south, the man left the park through the main gate. Once outside, Bianca kept to the shadows on the opposite side of the road, avoiding the pools of light from the street lamps. She noticed the ground was twinkling with frost and took care not to slip as she crossed the market square, following the stranger across the bridge over the canal.

As she approached the city's industrial district, Bianca grew more and more worried. She didn't know this area. What if she got lost and couldn't find her way back?

But she knew in her bones that this odd man was

somehow connected to what had happened to Finn, Sophie and Casper. The memory of his crocodile smile made her hands curl into fists. *I can't turn round now*, she thought.

Every building she passed was a warehouse or a factory, and Bianca realized with growing horror that nobody lived in this part of the city. It was busy during the day, but at night it was a ghost town. If she cried out for help, there would be nobody to hear her. And so she took extra care, hiding in doorways, ducking behind walls and tiptoeing as she trailed the mysterious man.

Bianca was hiding behind a dustbin, peering over the top, when the towering man sneezed. It was the strangest sound, like a nasal roar. Although she didn't feel it, a breeze must have caught the hem of the man's coat because it billowed and rose, as if the sneeze had been powerful enough to blow it off. Bianca double blinked. She could have sworn that, just for a second, she had glimpsed four feet!

'Quilo!' the man said, chiding himself as he approached a dilapidated old building with broken windows.

Slipping out from behind the bin, Bianca sidled along a low fence between the pavement and the factory, getting as close as she dared. The hairs on her body were tugging her skin into a petrified pattern of goosebumps. The closer she got to the factory, the colder she felt. Here, the ground was covered in a thick layer of ice. She pulled her coat close to her body, wrapping her arms across her chest. She was shivering. She read the peeling wooden sign outside the run-down building.

DOWNY FALLS
BOOKBINDING FACTORY

'We're here!' boomed the stranger, and Bianca jumped as his coat shot up into the air again, like a carrier bag caught by a strong gust of wind. A pyramid of children was standing beneath it!

Rising to look over the fence, she saw, at the bottom of the pyramid, a boy and a girl dressed in grey, with grey hair and grey eyes. They looked like twins, different only in that one wore a dress and had long hair. Bianca guessed from their size that they were about the same age as Finn. Standing on their shoulders was a chunkier boy wearing a bearskin. He had cherubic cheeks and his ruddy face was framed by a tangled mass of brown curls. He was only the height of a ten-year-old, but of the four he looked the oldest. Sitting on his shoulders was a pale child as thin as a willow sapling, dressed in an old-fashioned white suit, like a page at a wedding, with white hair tied back in a ponytail under the top hat.

The child dressed in white used the shoulders of the boy in the bear suit for purchase and somersaulted to the ground, catching the top hat as it fell and putting it back on.

The twins ducked, stepping backwards in unison, dropping the boy in the bear suit on the ground. He landed flat on his back, expelling all the air from his lungs.

Bianca felt a thrill of terror as her hair was blown back from her face by a sudden gale. The trees behind her shook and broken shards of glass dropped from the factory windows and hit the ground with a crash. She clamped her hands over her mouth to stop herself from crying out, and dropped back down behind the fence, trembling.

Who were these children?

Crawling along the ground, her muscles rigid with fear, she found a hole in the fence to peer through.

The short, stocky boy in the bear suit jumped to his feet. 'Pitter!' His joyful voice roared as he grabbed the shoulders of the grey boy. 'Patter!' He looked at the grey girl. 'You rats!'

Bianca thought his eyes too old for his cherubic face. He looked as if he'd seen terrible things. There were silver streaks in his chestnut mane.

'You are always so loud, Quilo!' Pitter exclaimed.

'Yes, you huff and bellow and billow!' Patter echoed.

'We should not be out here, making all this noise,' the deathly pale child said, looking around.

Bianca had thought the figure in the top hat a man because of the dark glasses, height and clothes, but she realized that this child, who'd been the face of the stranger, might be a girl or a boy. They were about the same height as she was and, from the way they spoke, the leader of the gang.

'We could be seen!' the child snapped.

'Or in a word . . .' Pitter looked pointedly at Quilo.

'. . . overheard.' Patter finished her twin's sentence.

Quilo stuck out his tongue at the twins, blowing the longest, loudest and most powerful raspberry that Bianca had ever witnessed. It blew the grey pair backwards, right off their feet, sending them rolling across the ground.

'Enough, Quilo! Pitter, Patter, get inside.' The child in white herded them towards the door into the factory.

'It's not my fault, Jack,' Quilo said, putting on puppy eyes. 'I can't help it.' A mischievous grin lit up his face. 'It's my nature to be impulsive.' He waggled his eyebrows and Jack tried not to smile. 'Now, my frosty sibling –' Quilo reached up, putting an arm round Jack's shoulder – 'how about giving us some glass for those windows?' He pointed at the factory. 'Smarten the place up a bit.'

'So that you can shatter them again with one of your tricks?' Jack's voice was accusatory.

'I don't know what you mean,' Quilo blustered. 'I thought it might stop people hearing what we're up to.'

Jack paused, considering the suggestion, then tugged at the gloved fingers of their right hand. 'That's a good idea.'

Bianca's mouth dropped open as the glove slipped

off, revealing the hand beneath. Each jagged digit was extraordinarily long, whalebone-white, and tapered into a sharp needle of ice, like a snowflake. Jack placed the alien hand on the brickwork of the factory. A crackling sound ricocheted up the empty street. Bianca held her breath as every vacant window grew a fresh pane of glass. It spread like spilt water across the empty casements. In under a minute all the factory windows were repaired.

'Wonderful!' Quilo clapped.

'*Shhh*. If we are discovered, our mission will fail,' Jack said, withdrawing the hand and putting the glove back on. 'You know we cannot afford to fail.'

'Don't fret. Do not fear,' Pitter poked his head round the door.

'It won't be long. Our time is near.' Patter's head appeared above her brother's.

'The winter is coming.' Quilo suddenly looked serious. 'We will save our sister.'

Jack replied with a nod, then glanced up and down the street, before following the others into the factory and shutting the door.

Bianca slumped onto the icy ground, giddy with relief that she hadn't been caught.

6

THE BOOKSELLER

Bianca ran all the way back to the park. She couldn't tell if it was her imagination or because she was running, but it felt like the further she got from the four strange children, the warmer it became. Her mind was a blizzard of questions, whirling and dancing, so that she couldn't focus on any one thing or catch any answers.

Who were they? What were they doing? Why were they going about the city pretending to be a man? What was wrong with that kid's hand? Where had the glass in the windows come from?

Bianca knew she'd been gone for a long time and was worried her parents had woken up and discovered she was missing. They were so distressed about Finn;

she didn't want to make it worse. When she finally stumbled into the rose garden, breathless and worn out, she was relieved to find her parents still fast asleep on the bench. A gentle snore was rising from her father's lips.

Taking the spare sleeping bag from the tent, Bianca climbed into it and wriggled under her dad's arm. She could hear his heart beating. It was a comforting sound. It soothed the frightened thoughts that buffeted her brain. As she warmed up, her eyes closed, and her breath fell into sync with her father's.

'Bianca, my love, wake up,' her dad called softly, and she floated out of darkness. 'Mum's going to take you home.'

Bianca blinked her eyes open, remembering she was in the park. The sky was the colour of mushrooms, the dawning sun obscured by the thick snow clouds. Her legs were stiff. It was very cold. She saw a frill of frost on the rose bushes. Her mum helped her to her feet and a police officer escorted them out of the park and into a car, before driving them home.

Taking her straight up to her bedroom, Bianca's mum tenderly removed her boots and tucked her into her bed fully dressed.

'Sophie and Casper have been frozen, Mum,' Bianca mumbled. 'They're from my school.'

'The police officer told me,' her mum replied in a whisper. 'It's not safe for you to be in the park, Bianca. That's why I've brought you home. Now, get some sleep.'

Bianca knew that nowhere was safe. Hadn't Finn been stolen from his own bed? But she didn't say this. She just nodded and closed her eyes, allowing the warmth of her own bed to envelop her.

The deathly pale Jack, with the snowflake hand and needle teeth, was waiting for her in her dreams, holding out a sparkling silver book. But every time she reached for it, it was whipped away and the wind laughed at her.

When Bianca awoke, she had a fire in her belly. Today she was going to get her hands on one of those silver books even if it killed her. Tomorrow she would have to go to school and there would be no time to investigate. She pulled her boots back on and clattered down the stairs.

Her mum was already up. She was sitting at the kitchen table drinking coffee. 'What would you like for breakfast?' she asked Bianca brightly. 'I've made banana bread.' One glance around the room told

Bianca that her mother had been cleaning for hours. Everything shone like new, and the room smelt of lemons.

'You baked banana bread?'

'Yes. I couldn't sleep.' Her mother looked into her coffee cup, which she was turning nervously in her hands. 'I didn't know what else to do.'

Bianca sat down, reaching for her mum's hand. 'I'm going to work out who did this to Finn, and Casper and Sophie, and then I'm going to find a way to unfreeze them.'

'You don't need to do that.' Her mum gave her a watery smile. 'You just keep yourself safe, Bianca. Don't go talking to strangers. The police are taking things much more seriously now that two more children are . . . in the park.'

'But I've got a lead. It's something to do with the silver book. Finn and Sophie both had one. I'll bet Casper did too.'

'Bianca, books can change what people think, and touch their hearts, but I don't see how they can freeze a person.' Her mother got to her feet. 'Now, how about I toast a slice of that banana bread for you and cover it in butter?'

Bianca nodded. She wasn't going to argue with her mum. As she ate her breakfast, she made lots of appreciative noises and praised her mother's baking, but it barely raised a smile.

'If you're going back to the park,' Bianca said, licking the melted butter from her fingers, 'can I go to the library? Mrs Dorcas will look after me, and it's cold in the park.'

'I don't see why not.' Her mum cleared away her plate. 'I'd feel happier knowing you were in a safe place.'

When Bianca opened the front door, the air that rushed to greet her was so cold that it stung to breathe in. There were two bottles of milk standing on her doorstep. Picking one up, she shook it. The creamy contents didn't move. It was frozen. *Winter has the power to transform a liquid into a solid,* she thought, and found her mind leaping to an image of her brother and her friends in the park. Her throat tightened and her eyes prickled as a sudden wave of fear and sadness threatened to overwhelm her. She shook herself, shoving the bottles on the hall table, inside the house, and closing the door roughly. She patted her coat pocket, checking her diary and pen were inside. She must concentrate on her investigation.

A neighbour was scraping frost off the windscreen of his car and talking to a woman a few doors down.

'Did you hear? Two more were discovered last night!' he said.

Bianca drew back into the porch, listening to their conversation.

'That's three children frozen now,' replied the woman.

'Yes! I mean, what are we supposed to do?'

'My sister's taking her children out of the city.'

'But the Christmas holidays are coming.'

'It's not safe here.'

'You think more children will be frozen?'

'Almost certainly.'

'What kind of a monster targets children!' the man exclaimed.

'I heard that the mayor has called for volunteers to patrol the streets at night. My Ron is joining up.'

'I hope they catch whoever is doing this soon.' The man opened his car door, signalling he had to go.

As Bianca walked down the path, she felt the woman staring at her.

I wish it would hurry up and snow, she thought, fastening her coat and putting on her gloves, ignoring the gawping neighbour. The ground was treacherously icy. She half walked, half slid to the library, losing her balance several times, but managing to catch herself before she fell.

Bianca had decided that as soon as she got hold of a silver book, she would take it to the police station and explain her theory, that it was somehow linked to the frozen children. The book was evidence.

No, it's not evidence, she thought suddenly. *It's a weapon!* She stopped walking as a worrying thought crossed her mind. *Or is it a trap?* What if she found a book and it imprisoned her in ice? Surely she would be able to resist its spell because she knew what it was. But what if she couldn't? Would she be frozen too?

'I won't read it,' she told herself, continuing on her way. 'I can't help Finn if I'm an ice statue.'

But what if it wasn't the reading that got you? What if it was looking at the pictures? Or maybe you didn't even need to look inside. What if just holding the book trapped you?

When I find one, I won't touch it, Bianca thought, looking at her gloved hands. *I'll keep my gloves on, put the book into a bag and wrap it up tight.* She always carried a folded-up bag in her pocket, for picking up other people's litter.

When she got to the library, Bianca found the giant wooden doors closed. She tried the handle. They were locked. She saw the sign beside the door, CLOSED ON SUNDAY, and her heart sank. She'd been so caught up in events that she'd forgotten the library didn't open today.

She dropped down, sitting on the steps, the wind gone from her sails. *At least*, she consoled herself, *if the library is closed, no one can get a silver book today.*

No silver books meant no more frozen children.

But it didn't help Finn. He'd been frozen for two nights now. How long could he remain that way and survive? She immediately shook the horrible thought from her head. She mustn't think like that. Instead, she thought about the four strange children she'd seen last night at the factory. She suspected they had something to do with the silver books, although none of them had been carrying one. But she remembered the victorious smile on Jack's face at the sight of poor frozen Casper. She was certain they had something to do with that.

A girl with a pixie crop and a wide smile skipped past the library steps. Bianca sprang to her feet. The girl was holding on to her mother's hand and under her other arm she was carrying a silver book.

Recognizing her as Gwen Olsen, who often played with Finn in the park, Bianca called out, running after her.

'Gwen, wait!'

Her mother stopped and turned. When she saw who'd called her daughter, her expression changed to a pitying smile. 'Bianca!'

Having learned her lesson with Sophie, Bianca darted forward and grabbed the silver book under Gwen's arm. She yanked it away.

But Gwen had been gripping the book tightly. When Bianca yanked it, she pulled Gwen off her feet. As she fell, Gwen yelped and knocked the book from Bianca's hands. She threw herself on top of the book on the pavement. 'It's mine!'

'Bianca!' Gwen's mum looked shocked. 'What on earth are you doing?'

'You mustn't let her read that book!' Bianca cried. 'It's dangerous.' She turned to the five-year-old girl. 'Gwen,' she said, trying to soften her voice, as if talking to a frightened cat. 'You know me. I'm Finn's sister.' Gwen's eyes grew wide. 'Did you hear what happened to him?'

'He got turned into ice,' Gwen replied.

'Finn had a silver book like yours. He read it on the day he was frozen. That book is a trap. I think that if you read it you will turn into ice too.'

'That's enough, Bianca!' Gwen's mother stepped protectively in front of her wide-eyed daughter. 'You're scaring her.'

Gwen hugged the glinting book to her chest, a feverish look in her eyes.

'I'm sorry about what happened to your brother,' Mrs Olsen said, 'but you can't go around frightening little children. Everyone is scared enough as it is. If you want a book so badly, then go to the bookseller in the market – he's got a box of them. It's where Gwen got hers.'

'What I'm saying about the book is true, Mrs Olsen! You must believe me. Please don't let Gwen read it. Please!'

The number 73 pulled up at the library bus stop. Mrs Olsen grabbed her daughter and ushered her on board, clearly in a hurry to get away from Bianca. As the doors closed, Gwen waved, but Bianca was already running towards the market square.

She sprinted past the cathedral. Its bells were ringing to signal the end of morning service. She sped by City Hall and arrived gasping in the square. There was a market every weekend. On Saturdays it was a food market, with fresh fruit, veggies, fish and meat, but on Sunday it was antiques, curiosities, old clothes and second-hand books.

The market traders were wrapped up in thick coats and scarves. Gloved hands clutched steaming cups of coffee. There weren't many people shopping. It was too cold.

Bianca spotted three trestle tables stacked with books. A short man wearing a flat cap and waxed jacket stood beside it.

'Excuse me,' Bianca said, approaching him. 'Are you the bookseller?'

'Indeed I am, young miss.'

'I'm looking for a book.'

'What's it called?'

'I don't know, but it's got a silver cover.'

'Do you know how many people think I'll know which book they're talking about if they just tell me the colour of the cover?' He chuckled. 'I'll need a bit more to go on than that. Who's it by?'

'I don't know, but you sold a copy to a five-year-old girl just now. She has short brown hair.'

'I didn't! I haven't made a sale all morning. It's too frosty for people to take off their gloves and reach into their wallets.'

'But her mother said you had a box of books,' Bianca cried. 'She said . . .'

'Oh! Them!' The bookseller pointed to a cardboard box on the floor. 'She must have taken it from there.'

Under the table was a box with a sign pinned to the side saying FREE BOOKS FOR CHILDREN. Bianca dropped to her knees and rummaged through it.

'There isn't anything worth much in there, but, if a child likes something, their grown-up usually feels obliged to buy a book off the table.' The bookseller sounded pleased with his clever ruse.

'Did you put a silver book in here?' Bianca asked, riffling through tatty board books, comics and dog-eared paperbacks, her heart slowly sinking.

'I don't think so, but, if I'm honest, I don't pay much attention to the box until it's looking empty.'

Bianca drew back. There were only ordinary books in the box. It struck her as odd that there was a scattering of hailstones under the table, but her desperate search drove all other thoughts from her head. She was too late. Once again, the mysterious silver book had eluded her.

7

A DEADLY DECEMBER

Bianca couldn't face going to the park and seeing Finn after she'd failed to stop Gwen from taking a silver book home. She dreaded hearing the news that she feared was coming. Tonight, after midnight, little Gwen would be found frozen.

Frustrated that she had nothing to show for her efforts, Bianca returned home. Finding the house was empty, she went into the kitchen and threw herself into a chair at the table, dropping her head into her hands. It felt as if there were something impossibly big and powerful behind what was happening in the city. She knew the weather wasn't something a person could control, but she couldn't shake the feeling that the wintry spell of the past two days had something to do with what was going on. She had never known a December cold enough to freeze milk.

She rubbed her hands together to warm up her icy fingers, then pulled her diary from her coat pocket. Nothing added up to much in her head – her mind was buried in an avalanche of thoughts – but, perhaps, if she set everything down on paper, she might see a pattern or have an idea. Bianca thought she might draw a map of the city too, marking the places where strange things had happened. She'd seen people do that on TV shows. She wanted to know who or what she was up against. It felt as if she were chasing someone who was invisible.

Opening her diary, she turned to the first week of December, reading over the scraps of notes she'd made so far. She considered the strange poem that was carved into the ice pedestals that Finn and Casper stood on. She hadn't got close enough to see if it was also on Sophie's.

DARK DAYS GROW EVER WARMER.
WINTER'S ON THE RUN.
ICE BECOMES A LIQUID,
BENEATH A SEARING SUN.
WHEN THE SEASONS ALTER,
SOMETHING MUST BE DONE.
WITH THE HEARTS OF CHILDREN,
WINTER WILL LIVE ON.

What did it mean? She read it out loud, but it made no sense to her. She didn't like the last line. It made her shudder.

In the box marked the first of December, she wrote FINN FROZEN. Then, in the box for the second, she wrote SOPHIE & CASPER FROZEN. Tomorrow would be Monday the third. Her pen hovered over the empty box for a second, and then she wrote GWEN FROZEN. Would there be more ice children? Had there been more than one silver book in the bookseller's box? A dreadful thought popped into her head.

One child had been frozen on the first of December, two on the second. Would there be three children frozen on the third? And four the day after? That would mean there were at least three silver books, possibly more! What about the next day and the day after that? Would there be five on the fifth and six on the sixth? Her mind reeled at this terrifying idea.

When will it stop?

What if it doesn't?

Bianca looked down at her diary, taking in the dates. She felt dizzy with the certainty that, like a deadly advent calendar, each day would reveal more frozen children, unless someone could put a stop to it.

Getting up, she tore a blank sheet from an A4 pad

on the sideboard and brought it back to the table. On it, she drew a crude map of the city, marking the outlines of the park. She wrote FINN in the rose garden, SOPHIE in the bandstand and CASPER by the boating lake. She wondered where Gwen would be found, and shivered. Sketching in the circular library to the right of the park, she moved her hand down to add in the cathedral, City Hall and the market square. She marked the place where the bookseller had been with an X, then added two Xs to the library. These were places she was certain children had picked up silver books.

What she didn't know was how the books had got to the library or into the bookseller's box. She suddenly remembered the hailstones she'd seen under his table. There had been hailstones around the base of Finn's pedestal.

Are they a clue?

She wrote HAILSTONES down in her diary.

On her map, on the south side of the market square, she drew the canal and the bridge that crossed it, marking the industrial area and, beyond it, the docks. Inside the industrial area she drew a little factory.

Bianca remembered she'd written the name of the factory in the back of her diary. She turned the pages and stared at the words: DOWNY FALLS BOOKBINDING FACTORY.

Her pen hovered above her map.

'It's a bookbinding factory!' she gasped.

How had she missed that?

She had been so intrigued by the peculiar children pretending to be a man, that she'd failed to see what was right in front of her face! The factory made books!

Bianca thought of Jack with the strange hand and how glass had magically appeared in the broken windows. Jack and the boy in the bearskin had spoken about being on a mission. What was it? Were they working for someone? Who could it be?

She drew a circle around Downy Falls. Was this the place the silver books were coming from? Bianca felt certain it must be, and that the four peculiar children had something to do with it!

8

THE MAYOR'S MEETING

Bianca was so deep in thought that the noise of a key in the front door made her jump.

'Dad!' she exclaimed peering down the hall.

'I've come back for a change of clothes,' he explained. 'I thought you were at the library.'

'It was closed. I forgot. It's Sunday.'

'Oh. The mayor has called a meeting in City Hall this afternoon.' He went to the fridge and took out a tub of leek-and-potato soup, tipping it into a pan and turning on the gas. 'He's going to lead a discussion about the frozen children. People are frightened. We need to come together and decide what should be done.'

Bianca thought about little Gwen. 'Can I come

with you to the meeting?'

'Yes, if you want to.' Her father looked surprised. 'It might be boring and . . . well, a bit upsetting.'

'I want to come. I need to tell people about the silver books.'

'Silver books?'

'Yes. Finn had one, and I saw Sophie Lilley with one before she was frozen—'

'Bianca.' Her dad shook his head. 'Now is not the time for one of your tall tales. Other people won't humour you like your mother and I do. This situation is deadly serious.'

Bianca's mouth hung open. 'This isn't a story,' she protested.

'I'm making soup.' He turned to face the cooker. 'Do you want some?'

'Dad, you have to believe me.'

'Bianca.' Her dad's voice softened as he saw she was getting upset. 'Let's say you're right and this book has something to do with the frozen children.'

'I am,' Bianca insisted. 'It does.'

'Then can you tell me *how* a book carried Finn to the park and froze him?' He stirred the soup silently for a moment. 'Because that's what I keep asking myself. How did Finn go from lying safe in his bed, fast asleep, to being in the park, encased in ice?'

'I . . . I don't know,' Bianca admitted. She wondered whether she should tell him about the four children in the bookmaking factory disguising themselves as a man in a top hat, but knew it sounded made up. He'd never believe her. 'Perhaps it's magic,' she suggested weakly.

'Bianca, I don't believe in magic and dragons and wizards.' Her dad smiled sadly. 'Those things only exist in books and stories – else I'd put on a suit of armour and charge about slaying dragons until someone gave us Finn back.'

When the soup was hot, he poured it into two bowls and put them down on the table.

Bianca took the spoon and the bread he offered her. She agreed with her dad. Magic did exist in books, especially silver glittering ones.

They ate in silence.

'I need to tidy myself up before the meeting.' Her dad finished his soup by mopping his bowl clean with a hunk of bread. 'I won't be long.'

The image of Gwen clutching her glittering book was at the forefront of Bianca's mind as she finished her soup. She needed to get the message to everyone in the city not to let their children read the silver stories. If she went to the meeting and told all the grown-ups that Gwen Olsen had a cursed book and would become one of the frozen children at midnight, and then it came true, they'd have to believe her.

As Bianca and her dad walked down the street, she noticed the drop in temperature had changed the sound of the city. Ice made porous surfaces solid, so that they reflected noises, creating eerie echoes. People's footsteps sounded loud and sharp. It made Bianca jumpy. She kept looking over her shoulder, half expecting to see a towering figure wearing a long dark coat and top hat.

When they reached City Hall, a crowd was gathered outside. People drew back as Bianca and her father arrived, letting them pass. Anxious parents clutched their children tightly. She saw fear and pity in their eyes. Theirs was one of the frozen families.

The clock chimed. People were seated. The mayor, dressed in his official garb of red coat and chunky gold chain, stepped onto the stage, flanked by two officers. He raised his hands and the murmuring crowd fell silent.

Bianca looked around. The hall was stuffed with concerned people. For a second, right at the back, she thought she caught a glimpse of a black top hat, and her stomach squirmed with alarm, but then it was gone. Were the strange children here? She grabbed her dad's hand, suddenly deciding she would tell him about them, but the mayor began speaking.

'I have called this meeting to discuss the three frozen children,' the mayor said, looking at the silent crowd. 'I am a parent of little ones. Like you, I am alarmed and want to understand what is going on.'

'What's happening to our children?' a woman called out.

'We don't know.' The mayor shook his head. 'However, although the children are frozen, the doctor assures me that they are all alive. We have medical specialists coming to town tomorrow to advise on the best route forward.'

'What can we do to keep our children safe?' asked a man.

'Nothing,' a low rumbling voice replied, and Bianca saw a man with the same features as his son but whose head was crowned with silver hair. It was Casper's dad, Mr Rimes. 'My doors and windows were locked.' He shook his head. 'And still my boy was taken from me.'

'Is it a disease?' one parent shouted at the mayor. 'Is it infectious? Should we be looking for a cure?'

'I need to know how I can protect my babies!' a mother cried.

The meeting was getting out of control. Bianca knew she had to say something quickly before it collapsed into chaos. Her heart was racing as she rose from her seat. Her father looked puzzled as she walked to the front of the hall and stood before the stage, facing the crowd. Her lungs felt tight and her mouth was dry but she said, as loudly and as clearly as she could, 'My name is Bianca Albedo. I know what made my brother freeze.'

The crowded hall fell silent. Suddenly she felt every eye upon her.

'What did she say?' someone near the front whispered.

'I know what froze my brother,' Bianca said. 'It was a silver book.'

'Did she say she'd been reading a book?' came another whisper.

'Finn was reading a silver book that he got from the library the night he was frozen—'

'Which book?' someone asked.

'I don't know what it's called, but—'

'Of course! It was a book that did it!' A well-meaning woman at the front winked at Bianca. 'A spell book probably. Am I right?'

Several people sniggered.

'Don't be cruel,' someone hissed. 'She lost her little brother.'

'Finn's not dead!' Bianca snapped, feeling herself getting hot. 'He's frozen!'

'We should be trying to thaw the children,' a voice called out, and there was a murmur of approval at this idea.

'How do we do that?'

'We could build fires at their feet!'

'We could spray them with hot water!'

And suddenly all the adults were calling out, talking over one another, about ways to warm the children.

In a panic, Bianca could feel her moment slipping away. 'If you don't believe me,' she cried over the clamour, 'tonight more children will be frozen and one of them will be—'

A voice bellowed, drowning her out. 'Mr Mayor, what do you think about thawing the children?'

With a lurch of fear, Bianca recognized the bellowing voice. It belonged to the boy in the bear suit. The one called Quilo. She saw the towering figure in dark glasses and top hat standing to the side of the hall. She glared at it, gritting her teeth angrily. Jack's chin lifted. Bianca was determined not to be stared down. But as the dark glasses lowered, she faltered, suppressing a gasp, as she saw that Jack's eyes were like two opal stones, with no pupils or irises, utterly unreadable.

Chilled to the very marrow of her bones, Bianca turned away, suddenly afraid, hurrying back through the concerned people of the city.

When she reached her dad, he was on his feet, shouting angrily, 'I will not allow anyone to build a fire anywhere near my son!'

Everyone was hollering and calling out. No one was listening. The mayor had his hands up, trying to instil order.

Bianca took in all their frightened and angry faces and knew they weren't going to listen to what she had to say. She was on her own. And every day that she failed to stop the four oddball kids with their silver books more of the city's children would turn up frozen in the park.

'Let's get out of here, Dad,' she said, pulling at his arm. 'I want to go home.'

9

DOWNY FALLS

When they got home, Bianca's dad suggested she get into bed and rest. 'You've got school tomorrow, Bianca . . .'

'School? I can't go to school. I need to help Finn,' Bianca said angrily, and the concerned expression on her dad's face intensified. 'Didn't you see what was happening back there, in the hall? That man in the top hat stopped me from explaining about the silver book, and he's not really a man at all! He's four children on each other's shoulders. I saw them go into an old book factory last night and one of them has hands like giant snowflakes and . . .'

'I'm sorry, Little Bee,' her dad said, using a pet name he hadn't for years. 'I think your mother and I have been so worried about Finn we've failed to think about how all of this is affecting you. Perhaps it would be a good idea for you to go and visit your granny.'

'No!' Bianca's insides lurched.

'You love visiting her, and you'd even get to miss a bit of school. Think of it like a little holiday, just until we've worked out how to help Finn.'

'I want to help Finn too. I promised him.'

'What's happened to Finn has upset you deeply. I can see that.' Dad put an arm round her, hugging her head to his chest. 'It's only natural for you to use your wonderful imagination to try and make sense of all this.' His voice was kind, but Bianca wanted to cry. 'You don't really think that magic books are freezing children, and that an adult with a top hat is really four children who live in a factory – do you?'

Bianca was unsure how to reply. If she said yes, Dad would send her away and she wouldn't be able to help Finn, but she refused to pretend she'd made it up. 'I don't want to go to Granny's. I want to be near Finn, and you and Mum.'

'I'll discuss it with your mother tonight.'

'You have to believe me,' Bianca said, trying again. 'Tonight, at midnight, Gwen Olsen will be found frozen in the park. I think there will be two other children there too, but I don't know who they'll be . . .'

'*Shhh* now, my Little Bee. You're upsetting yourself. You need to sleep.' He placated her as if she were four years old, taking her upstairs, removing her shoes, helping her put on her nightie and pulling the covers up to tuck her in.

Bianca wanted to shout at him to believe her, but knew it wouldn't help. She didn't want to hurt his feelings. He was already so sad. Once in bed, she turned towards the wall and closed her eyes, pretending to go to sleep.

It was down to her to stop Jack, Quilo, Pitter and Patter. No one was going to help her. No one believed her. As she lay there with her eyes closed, her father watching her from the end of her bed, Bianca formulated a plan.

When Bianca woke up it was dark. Her father was gone from her room. Picking up her alarm clock, she saw it was 4.30 in the morning. She slipped out of bed and got dressed as swiftly and silently as she could. She found her school uniform and hid it inside her duvet cover, then wrote a note to her parents saying that she'd got up early and gone to school. She propped it up on her desk. Pulling on her boots and coat, Bianca checked she had her gloves and diary, and then crept along the landing to her brother's room.

She had laid Sposh on the pillow where Finn had left him. Bianca untied the red scarf from round the rabbit's neck, retying it round her own wrist as a good-luck charm. She needed luck for what she was about to do.

Taking one stair at a time, she reached the front door making the minimum of sound. She didn't hear anyone stirring. Reaching up to the coat rack, she grabbed her woolly beret and a scarf, putting them on before she opened the front door.

Stepping out into the street felt like entering a magical world. The sky was black, but the ground, the shrubs and the cars had grown a fur coat of frost, tinted yellow by streetlights. The pavement was buttered with a thick glassy smear of ice. After Bianca's feet had gone from under her several times, she gave up walking and slid along as if she were ice skating. She knew exactly where she was heading. Only one place held the answers to her questions. Downy Falls.

There wasn't a car on the road, or a person in sight. As she crossed the bridge over the canal, entering the industrial district, she felt a further drop in temperature.

When the bookbinding factory appeared in the distance, the tumbledown building was lit from inside by a turquoise light.

In the time it had taken her to walk there, the sky

had warmed from black to the colour of an aubergine's skin.

Taking a steadying breath, Bianca crept along the street, bent double, and ran swiftly through the gateless entry posts of Downy Falls. Ignoring the path to the door, she scouted around the perimeter of the building. Under a row of windows, she found a stony flowerbed. In it was a wizened shrub, devoid of sap and life, and an equally dead lilac tree. Wriggling until she was in the nook between the dead plants and the factory wall, she settled into her hiding place, hoping that none of the strange children would venture round this side of the building.

Kneeling up, Bianca peeped through the window into the factory. She had a blurry and imperfect view. The glass reminded her of a frozen stream she had

once seen. The bubbling water had been transformed into a glassy solid, circles of air trapped beneath its surface.

The factory appeared to be abandoned. She couldn't see anyone inside. She listened but heard no movement. Summoning her courage, she rose a little higher and cupped her hands around her eyes to see better.

Through the window she saw a cavernous room with a concrete floor. The otherworldly turquoise light seemed to radiate from a big machine that wound through the space like a snake, its tongue a black conveyor belt. The machine looked old. Some parts were spotted with rust, some looked broken and others appeared to be new and made of silver. At the back, Bianca could make out a staircase up to a walkway that led to three doors. She wondered if the children lived here, if the rooms were bedrooms, or just offices.

Sinking back into her hiding place, Bianca considered how long it might be before the children arrived, or woke up, and went about their business. She sat, watching the aubergine sky lightening slowly by degrees. She hoped her parents had found her note, although, she realized, when she didn't turn up to school, they'd get a phone call. She didn't want them to think she'd been frozen, although once Dad learned that Gwen was in the park, she hoped he would realize what she'd told him was true, and understand why she'd left the house before he got up. Her investigation was important.

There was a sudden blaze of white light inside the factory and Bianca risked a quick peep in through the window. The middle door on the raised walkway was open. The light coming from inside the room was blinding.

Pitter and Patter danced out, running to the iron staircase, tapping their feet as they ran down two steps and hopped up one. Quilo followed, standing at the top of the stairs with his hands on his hips, waiting for them to finish their routine. Then he beamed as if an idea had struck him, and, turning, he jumped backwards onto the railing and slid down the banister past the tap-dancing pair as Jack emerged and closed the door, shutting off the bright light.

Not wishing to be seen, Bianca ducked, blinking to adjust her eyes.

'Do we have the books?' Bianca heard Jack ask, and she immediately popped back up, hoping to see a silver book.

'I have two . . .' replied Pitter, pointing at a grey bag slung across his chest.

'. . . I have two too!' Patter added, pointing at her bag.

'Why must I always be the stomach?' Quilo grumbled, holding out the long black coat to Jack.

'You are the lungs,' Jack corrected him, pulling the dark glasses from a pocket and putting them on.

'We don't complain about being the legs . . .' Patter said.

'. . . even though your farts stink like bad eggs,' Patter added, and they both hooted with laughter.

Quilo harrumphed, turning his back on the twins, standing with his feet astride, waiting for Jack to put his arms into the long black coat. Once dressed, Jack leapfrogged neatly onto Quilo's shoulders.

Pitter and Patter stood side by side, an arm locked around each other's shoulders, and bent their legs. Quilo took hold of both their outstretched arms and walked up their legs with Jack on his shoulders. Bianca marvelled at their acrobatics, thinking that Quilo must be very strong unless Jack weighed next to nothing. Quilo sat down on their linked shoulders, between Pitter and Patter's heads.

Jack smiled, fastening the coat around them, and the creepy man-sized figure lolloped forward.

'Now remember,' Jack said. 'We are to keep watch for that girl, Bianca Albedo. She nearly ruined everything at the meeting yesterday.'

'She's trouble,' Patter's muffled voice said.

'Danger doubled,' Pitter agreed.

'Oh, poo!' Quilo huffed, and the belly of the coat ballooned. 'She ran away as soon as you looked at her.'

'The bond of love the humans share is hazardous to our plan,' Jack said. 'It is powerful and triggers memories. Whatever happens, we cannot let Bianca Albedo get her hands on one of our special books.'

'Then we'll stay away from the library.' Quilo's voice came from inside the coat. 'She knows about that place.'

'Oh, I have a much better place to give out our books than the library.' Jack smiled. 'This morning we're going to distribute our beautiful presents to the keen children who arrive first at the school gates.'

And with that the towering figure lurched out of the factory.

10

BOOKBINDING

Peering around the corner of the building, Bianca felt a fizz of panic as she watched the tall, dark figure tottering down the road. What should she do? Should she race ahead of them and warn the parents at the school gates? The disbelieving faces from last night's meeting filled her mind. No. It wouldn't work. They thought she was mad with grief, and she was meant to be going to school herself.

Bianca couldn't stop the strange children from giving out their books, but she could get evidence about what they were doing and take it to the police. Then people would have to listen.

She thought about the things Jack and the others had said. It frightened her that they knew her name, but she took strength from the fact that they thought she was dangerous. They had said she was trouble, that she could ruin their plan, which made her all the more determined to do so.

The sun had risen. The day was lighter, though it barely felt any warmer. After waiting for a minute, to make sure the strange children weren't going to come back, Bianca ran to the factory door and tried the handle.

It was locked. She was going to have to break in. Rushing back to the window, she pressed her nose to the glass, double-checking that the coast was clear. When she pulled back, the skin of her nose had briefly stuck to the cold glass. Taking off her glove she touched the window. 'It's not glass!' Bianca exclaimed. 'It's ice!'

Taking a large flint from the flowerbed, she smashed at the ice until she'd made a hole big enough to climb through.

Dropping onto the factory floor, Bianca shivered. The inside of Downy Falls felt like a refrigerator. Looking around, she saw colourful graffiti tags and patterns decorating the mottled concrete walls. One or two adventurous plants had sprouted through the floor, their stems now bowing, weighed down by crystals of ice. She cautiously approached the machine

that took up most of the floor. To her it seemed like a sleeping sea serpent that might, at any second, wake up and devour her.

She peered into the mouth from which

the conveyor belt extended like a black tongue, but there was no sign of any silver books. She carefully examined each section of the machine, but found no clue about the books it made. She looked around. You couldn't make a book out of nothing. Where was the paper? Where was the ink?

A tiny white flake drifted past her eyes, and Bianca looked up, startled to see that a portion of the factory roof was missing, only skeletal iron beams remaining. Beyond them the thick low clouds were finally unloading their cargo of snow.

'Oh!' Bianca reached up and caught a flake on her gloved hand, then stuck out her tongue and caught another, feeling it turn to water. She couldn't remember the last time it had snowed before Christmas. There had been snow three years ago, in February, but it hadn't settled. Most of the time it was too warm for snow, but how Bianca loved the snow when it came. She tilted back her head, feeling the delicate flakes landing on her cheeks and eyelashes like the gentlest of kisses. Her soul lifted and she smiled to see the flakes getting heavier and falling faster. Reaching out her arms, she twirled – and then stopped. What was she doing? Now wasn't a time for playing! She was here to find evidence, and clues, anything that would break Finn and the others free from the ice that trapped them, and stop more children being frozen. She felt a hot flush of guilt.

She redoubled her search of the factory floor, looking under machinery, in every corner, but found nothing.

The only places she hadn't yet explored were the

rooms at the top of the iron staircase. Bianca felt a thrill of fear as she put her foot on the first step. What was waiting for her behind the three doors at the top? Taking care that each footstep landed as silently as a snowflake, she slowly climbed upwards. Glancing down, she felt a lurch of fear as she saw that the snow was telling tales on her. Her footprints were all over the factory floor, clearly visible in the fallen snow. She would have to wipe them away when she went back down.

Stepping onto the walkway, Bianca went to the first door and pressed her ear against it. She heard nothing. She tried the handle; it went all the way down. She opened the door a crack, peering in, and found herself looking at old tools and machine parts. An old dried-out mop and bucket stood in the corner. Everything was covered in cobwebs and the floor was carpeted with dust. It didn't look as if anyone had been inside this room for years.

Making her way to the second door, she saw an eerie wisp of smoke escaping from underneath it. When she tried the handle, she was surprised to find it was freezing cold. The door wouldn't open. It was locked. This was the room from which Jack and the others had emerged, backlit by a dazzling blaze of light. She listened, but heard nothing on the other side.

The third door was stiff, but she threw her weight against it as she pulled down the handle, and it popped open to reveal a room stacked with enormous rolls of paper for the bookmaking machine. This room, like the first, looked as if no one had been inside it for a long time.

Returning to the middle door, Bianca was certain that all the evidence she needed was on the other side. Running her fingers around the door frame, she searched for a key, but found none. She put her foot to the frame as she tugged and twisted the handle, but couldn't open it. She was about to run at the door, and throw her weight against it, when she heard approaching voices.

A crackle of panic in her chest exploded into fizzing fear. There was no time to get down the stairs and out of the window. She ran to the first door and slipped into the storeroom, leaving a thin crack so she could see out. She gasped as she remembered her telltale footprints in the snow. It was too late to do anything about them now.

The factory door opened.

'Well, that was easy. That was quick.'

'Jack, you were so dazzlingly slick.'

'It's easy to give a book to a schoolchild,' Jack said, jumping down and taking off the dark glasses to reveal those strange opal-like eyes, 'when they want it so desperately.'

Quilo did a forward roll off Pitter and Patter's shoulders, tumbling out of the coat and landing on his feet.

He began slapping his ballooned cheeks and chest in a rhythm, moving his lips into larger and smaller circles to change the pitch of the sound. Wiggling his bottom, he trumpeted a surprisingly high-pitched fart tune.

Pitter and Patter joined in, chuckling with glee as they tapped their feet on the concrete floor in time with Quilo. Starting slowly, they built up a pattern of taps that increased in pace and intricacy as they skipped across the floor. Bianca found her head was bobbing along in time as she marvelled at the speed with which their feet tapped, and inwardly rejoiced as they danced her footprints away.

A row of icicles hung from a railing beside the big machine. Jack flicked them and they rang like a glockenspiel.

'There'll be four tonight, and tomorrow five more, ' Pitter said, framing his face with jazz hands.

'One more today than ever before!' Patter declared.

'If you read, you know a book is a door,' Pitter sang out.

'It's production-line time. Hit the factory floor!' Patter spun round and pointed at the machine.

Jack finished the impromptu song by dragging their fingers along the icicles, making them sound like a wind chime.

From her hiding place, Bianca had a clear view of the children's movements around the factory. She took out her diary and pen and sketched them. She wrote JACK below the reedy figure with the ponytail and white suit, QUILO next to the chunky, cherubic boy in a bearskin, PITTER beneath the grey boy, and PATTER beneath the grey girl.

Now that Bianca was still, she was cold. She began shivering, which made it hard to control her pen, and, although she tried to carry on, the shivering became a juddering. Inside her head the rattle of her chattering teeth was terrifyingly loud. She clamped them together and put away her diary.

Had the factory got colder since the children had entered? It certainly felt like it.

She heard a clatter of metal and looked down to see Pitter and Patter laying out fine sheets of metal, flat on a table. Jack opened a pouch attached to their belt and carefully reached a long finger and thumb into it, drawing out something. Placing it on the palm of their free hand, Jack stroked it with the tip of one finger, staring at it with intense focus. Something glittered, but Bianca couldn't see what it was. Jack carefully laid it on one of the metal sheets, then took out another small object, and another, repeating the action five times.

'The mirror splinters are on,' Pitter declared.

'Now the plates are done,' Patter said excitedly.

Carefully lifting each of the sheets of metal, they slotted them into the big machine. Jack stood at the top of the printing press, at the opposite end to the conveyor belt, and laid their strange snowflake hands on a silver bar.

Bianca heard a sound like the creaking of old leather or the cracking surface of a frozen lake.

'Ready?' Pitter asked.

'Steady?' Patter asked.

'GO!' boomed Quilo.

There was a high-pitched whine as Jack spooled ice from their fingertips into the machine. It immediately clattered into action, printing the words and pictures from the silver plates onto pages of ice.

Bianca was shuddering violently with the cold now. Her fingers were blue. She pulled on her gloves, hugging her hands under her armpits. She suddenly realized why she'd not been able to find Finn's book. It had been made from ice! Once he'd read it, it had melted away, which explained the spilt water on the stack of books beside his bed. That's why there was no evidence of the books ever existing!

'Each night, more and more children are reading our bedtime story,' Jack said triumphantly as the first book came out on the conveyor belt.

'It's so heart-warming to see,' said Quilo, and the others seemed to find this very funny.

'It will please her,' Pitter said.

'It will ease her,' Patter agreed.

'We will make her strong again,' Jack proclaimed.

As the fifth book was being printed, Jack released their grip on the machine and watched as it was bound together and delivered by the conveyor belt.

Five glistening silver books lay there in a row. Bianca found herself leaning towards them. She wanted one so badly it hurt.

11

THE VANISHING WORLD

'**O**ur work is done for today,' Jack said, pulling their gloves back on. 'Time to go home and welcome our new brothers and sisters to Winterton.'

Winterton? Where is that? Bianca wondered.

Quilo pushed his shoulders back, sucked in the longest, most enormous breath and yelled, *'WAHOOOOOOOOOOOOOO!'* His breath hit the ground with such force that his body lifted high into the air.

Pitter and Patter linked hands, taking it in turns to whirl the other up and forward, their feet tapping as they danced. Bianca saw hail and sleet bouncing off the floor like rice thrown at a wedding. Remembering the hailstones she'd found at the foot of Finn's pedestal of ice, and under the bookseller's table, she craned her neck, trying to see where it was coming from.

As Quilo landed, he tipped his head back and let out a terrifying roar. It was an ancient, primal sound that shook Bianca's bones. She hugged her knees in terror as all the ice-glass windows in the factory exploded.

'Quilo!' Jack scolded, walking to the bottom of the iron staircase. 'Not the windows again! Someone could've heard that!'

'Whoops!' Quilo's face flushed. 'I couldn't help myself.'

'The North Wind howls and roars,' Pitter said.

'He's not meant to be indoors,' Patter pointed out.

'I give up!' Jack said with a shake of the head. 'I'll fix the windows when we come back tonight. Gather up the books and bring them.'

'Sorry.' Quilo followed Jack to the bottom of the stairs. 'It was an accident.'

'I've got two,' Pitter said, picking up a pair of books.

'I've two too,' Patter echoed, stuffing two of the silver books into her grey bag.

Bianca pushed the door shut as the four of them came up the stairs. She shrank back into the shadows of the store cupboard and held her breath. She heard the strange children passing and felt the cold intensify. Her skin was burning with it. There was a click and a clunk and then silence. She waited, straining her ears, but heard nothing. Eventually she cautiously opened the storage cupboard door and peeped out. There was no one on the walkway. Guessing they had gone into the middle room – the one they had come out of earlier – she tiptoed to the stairs as quietly as she could.

Stiff with the cold, Bianca could no longer feel her fingers or toes. She wondered how you knew if you had frostbite. *I need to get out of here and get warm*, she thought. She glanced about nervously. The factory was still. The window frames were empty. The machine lay glowing beneath her, and she gasped as her eyes caught a twinkle of silver. Inside the mouth of the machine, lying on the black conveyor belt was one of the silver books, sparkling like a star newly fallen from the night sky.

What was it doing there? Jack had instructed the others to bring the books with them. She remembered Quilo's apology for breaking the windows. Had he forgotten to pick up the last book? He might realize his mistake and return any second! This was her chance!

She was suddenly overcome with a tremendous desire to hold the book. It sang to her.

Bianca clattered clumsily down the staircase, unable to coordinate her frozen limbs. She ran to the conveyor belt, opening her arms as the book drew her towards it like a magnet. She saw a title: *The Vanishing World*.

'Wait!' she whispered to herself, her hand a centimetre from the enchanting cover. 'Don't touch it! Think of Finn. The book is trying to control you. Don't let it!'

But how could such a beautiful thing be bad? her mind replied. *You must have it! You deserve it. You've worked so hard to get it.*

'I will have it, but I won't touch it.' Bianca muttered as she pulled the plastic bag from her coat pocket and picked up the book between her gloved thumb and forefinger. A pleasant electric tingle raced up her arm, making her gasp. She dropped the book into the bag, holding it away from her. Her body cried out for her to touch it again. It felt wonderful.

'No,' she said firmly.

Hurrying away from Downy Falls with her stolen treasure, Bianca remembered what Jack had said: '*Whatever happens, we cannot let Bianca Albedo get her hands on one of our special books.*' She grinned. Well, she had one now and she was going to read it.

She stopped. No! That was the book talking. She *mustn't* read it. Her plan had been to take it to the police and that was what she must do. The book was evidence.

It was mid-morning by the time she reached the police station. She stood outside for a long time, an argument raging in her head. If she gave the book to the police, she'd never know what was inside it. And she *really* wanted to know. Curiosity was devouring her reason. She was becoming confused and indecisive. Before she'd got the book, she had decided that the right thing to do was give it to the police. Her thoughts had made sense to her then. Now she'd had to tell herself repeatedly not to listen to the call of the book, and so she decided she must trust herself.

Taking a deep breath, she shut the bag, which she'd opened without intending to, and marched up the steps before she could change her mind. She pushed through the swinging doors, going over to the desk where two police officers were on duty. 'My name is Bianca Albedo.' She put the bag on the counter. 'I'm here about the ice children in the park.'

'Good morning, Miss Albedo,' said one of the officers. 'Shouldn't you be at school?'

'Yes, I should,' Bianca agreed. 'But I must give you this book. It's evidence. The ice children all read this book the day before they got frozen. The book is what froze them.'

'Aren't you the girl from the meeting last night?' the other officer asked kindly. 'Your brother is Finn Albedo?'

'Er, yes.' Bianca faltered in the face of their understanding expressions.

'And this is the spell book you were telling everyone about, is it?' The first officer's voice had taken on a patronizing tone. He exchanged a glance with the other officer as he opened the carrier bag and looked inside. 'Oh, yes, that looks very . . . er . . . magical.'

Bianca was dismayed that they weren't taking her seriously.

She looked at the bag and felt a keen longing to take out the book and hold it. She leaned towards it, and wondered why it didn't seem to be having any effect on the police officers.

'Well, if this book is responsible for what happened to those children, perhaps we should arrest it.' The first officer chuckled, raising an eyebrow as he exchanged an amused look with his colleague.

'Yes.' The second officer put a hand on the bag and

looked down at Bianca as if she were six years old. 'You mustn't worry, Miss Albedo. We will put the naughty book in a prison cell where it can't freeze any more children.'

'No!' Bianca shouted, grabbing the bag back, spinning round and dashing out of the police station.

Snow was falling heavily, erasing the hard lines of the city, and Bianca found herself heading towards the park. There was a police officer at the main gate. She lowered her head and hurried past, making her way to the boating lake.

'Casper,' Bianca said, standing before her frozen friend. 'I don't know what to do. I have a silver book —' she waved the bag at him — 'but no one believes that it froze you.' Irritated by the hint of a smile on the left side of his mouth, she snapped at him. 'I don't know what you're looking so pleased about. Everyone is going out of their minds with worry.' She huffed. 'I thought you were the cleverest person I knew, until you got yourself frozen. Who am I supposed to talk to now? No one will listen to me!'

Fluffy flakes caught on her eyelashes, and she blinked them away.

Casper was still wearing his maddening smile, and it occurred to Bianca that Sophie had been beaming, and her brother looked serene. They were all happy to be frozen!

Her heart throbbed as she felt the sparkling book in the bag yearn for her to hold it, like a kitten wanting a cuddle.

What if being frozen wasn't bad? What if being frozen made you happy?

'I'm going to read it!' she said, willing Casper to defy her.

But Casper didn't move.

'Fine, then. I will!'

When Bianca got home, the house was empty. The afternoon was slipping away, school was finished now, and darkness was falling. She guessed her parents were in the park, with Finn, and felt disappointed that they'd believed her note and not realized she'd skipped school.

She went into the kitchen, putting the bag on the table with the book still inside it. She kept glancing at it, surprised by how much she wanted to hug it to her. Should she read the book? If she read it, she might learn what had happened to Finn. She watched the clock tick and tock, waiting. One of her parents would surely be back soon. She would show them the book. Then they would realize that she was right.

Time passed. The book called to her, again and again, until Bianca thought her heart would burst if she didn't pick it up.

Taking out her diary, Bianca wrote:

Dear Mum and Dad,

I have the silver book. I'm going to read it.

Tonight, I think I will be frozen, and you will find me in the park.

Don't be sad. I'm doing this to find out what happened to Finn.

If you get this note before midnight, please come and sit by my bed and hold my hand. I am scared.

I love you,

Bianca

She tore the page out of her diary, then put the diary back in her coat pocket, leaving the note on the kitchen table. Entering her bedroom, Bianca performed the habitual stroke of her favourite reindeer in the winter woodland wallpaper, then took the bag over to her bed. She clambered in, fully clothed, keeping her coat on. Taking a deep breath, she pulled off her gloves and removed the book from the bag.

As she touched it, the delightful tingling sensation

she'd felt before spread up her arms, to her shoulders and throughout her body. She felt her cramped muscles relax and the anxious coil in her chest melt away. She smiled at the shimmering crystalline cover, which reflected and refracted light, splitting it into tiny rainbows. It reminded Bianca of the frost fractals on her window. *The Vanishing World* was the most beautiful book she'd ever seen.

Opening the front cover, she saw a sparkling illustration of dancing snowflakes and a single sentence: *'There was once a time of harmony . . .'*

A deep thud, like a muffled bass drum, beat like a second heart inside her chest.

Somewhere in her head was the thought that she should shut the book, but she chased it away, greedily eating up every delicate detail on the page, the feather-like flourishes and snowflake swirls.

'There was once a time of harmony . . .'

The muffled drum boomed again inside her.

Illustrated snowflakes fell in graceful, scattered patterns around the deeply resonant words, and she fancied they were moving, creating a tinkling sound, like the notes on a distant piano.

A picture formed in Bianca's imagination, of a beautiful young queen with skin as translucent as ice and blood as pure as mountain streams. The queen

Within the illustration: *There was once a time of harmony*

longed to return to the world and blanket it in snow.

Delicate crystal chimes joined the tinkling piano in her head and the bass drum of her heart. The mischievous melody lifted Bianca's spirit, until she felt like a falcon soaring through the sky. Her skin prickled and her thoughts became as scattered as the snowflakes on the page. Her throat was dry, her forehead burning. She must open a window. She needed fresh air. How nice it would be to feel the cooling night breeze brushing against her wrists. Her blood was boiling. Her feet were walking. Down the stairs. Towards the front door. She saw her hand turn the latch.

It's happening. The thought flickered across her consciousness like a dragonfly in springtime, followed by the delicious sensation of being outside, like stepping into a pool on a hot summer's day.

She heard a familiar low voice speaking, but she couldn't focus on the words. The stars in the sky were winking at her. Outside was better than indoors, but still she was too hot. Her skin was on fire. She wanted to run, to feel the wind through her hair.

If only it would snow, she thought.

A voice spoke, close to her ear. '*I'm here, Bianca. I've got your hand.*'

I'm so hot, she thought, and looked down.

As if she'd commanded it, a block of ice was rising beneath her feet. *Ah, yes. That's better.*

She felt a cold wind and tried to reach her arms up to embrace it, but only one lifted. The other dragged at her side, but she didn't care. She smiled as the cooling breeze swirled around her. *This is heavenly. I could stay like this forever.*

A crackling, like the fizzle of electricity, incinerated all sound around her. The music had stopped, and silence spread like a pool of calm within her.

I wish the Snow Queen would come. She closed her eyes. *The world is too hot. How perfect it would be to have a snowy winter!* She smiled at this thought and wished hard. *Please come, Snow Queen. My heart longs for you. It's yours. Take it. Make it snow. Make it snow. Make it snow.*

12

FIRFROST FOREST

Although her eyes were closed, Bianca could see she was surrounded by a blazing bright light. *Am I dead?* she wondered, blinking her eyes open.

When she moved her arms, she found she was lying on her back in a soft eiderdown of powdered snow. The vast blue sky above her appeared to be held up by tall trees dressed in snowflake coats. Sunbeams bounced about like ping-pong balls. Bianca laughed with delight, swinging her arms and legs out in great arcs to make an angel.

Curiously, she found her right hand wouldn't swing as freely as her left. She lifted it, checking and turning it. It looked normal. Then she heard a man's voice, like a distant echo.

'I've got your hand Bianca. I won't let go.'

'Who's there?' she said, sitting up.

Bianca saw she was alone in a snowy clearing encircled by fir trees. She twisted onto all fours, letting out a startled yelp as she found herself nose to nose with a brown-eyed reindeer.

She crawled backwards, blinking. The reindeer drew back and blinked as well. Bianca tilted her head to the right, and so did the reindeer. She tilted it to the left and let out a laugh of surprise as the reindeer mirrored her once more.

'Well, who are you?' Bianca asked.

'Pordis,' said a girlish voice inside her head.

'Who said that?' Bianca looked around, alarmed.

'Pordis.'

Bianca leaped to her feet and the reindeer jumped backwards.

'Who's there?' Bianca stared into the shadows between the tree trunks.

'Pordis,' came the voice again.

'Show yourself, Pordis,' Bianca called out bravely, hoping she looked less scared than she felt.

The reindeer trotted around Bianca and stopped right in front of her.

Bianca looked questioningly at the reindeer. 'You are Pordis?'

The reindeer bowed its head.

'I am Bianca.'

'*Yes.*'

'And you are Pordis?'

'*Yes.*'

Bianca looked around to reassure herself that she was indeed having a private conversation with a reindeer.

'Where are we?'

'*Together,*' Pordis's soft voice said inside her head.

Bianca laughed, reaching out her hand and tentatively giving Pordis's coarse caramel coat a stroke. She sensed a bond with this creature. She knew it somehow. They were friends, companions.

'Yes, Pordis, but where are we together?'

'*Firfrost Forest.*'

'Firfrost Forest,' Bianca echoed, searching her mind for the story of how she came to be

here, but she drew a blank. She looked down at her clothes. She was wearing a coat and underneath it a purple knitted jumper that was far too big for her, with a white *B* on the front. A red ribbon of knitted wool was tied round her left wrist. When had she put these clothes on? Her brain gave her no answers.

'I was doing something,' she muttered. 'I'm sure I was. Something important.'

But, try as she might, Bianca couldn't remember anything about what had gone before this very moment. To her surprise, she didn't seem to mind.

Slipping her hands into her coat pockets, she found an orange diary and a pen.

'Are these mine?'

'*Are they your pockets?*' Pordis replied innocently.

Bianca laughed. 'Yes, they are!'

The orange diary was held shut with a piece of black elastic. Sitting down in the snow, Bianca opened it. She flicked through the early months of the year: January, February, March. They had dull and routine entries, things like 'Went to Casper's house' or 'Flute lesson'. Her brain seemed to know who Casper was and that she played the flute, but no further details. She was about to give up on the diary when a piece of paper fell out of the back. The page it fell from had drawings of four children on it: below the picture of a boy in a bearskin she had written QUILO, beneath a picture of a boy and girl holding hands she'd written PITTER and PATTER and the last figure wore a suit, and a top hat, and was called JACK. She unfolded the paper that had fallen from the diary and found she was looking at a crude map of a city. Had she drawn it? Was it something to do with how she'd got to Firfrost Forest? Suddenly she saw a name that made her heart vibrate like a plucked harp string: FINN.

'Finn,' she whispered. A vision bloomed in her head of a five-year-old boy with ash-blond hair, wide blue eyes, a snub nose and a toothless grin. He'd lost all four of his front teeth in the same week and had been so excited about the tooth fairy's visit. She remembered!

'*Finn?*'

'Oh, Pordis, Finn is my little brother. Something has happened to him.' She frowned. 'I don't remember what, but I think it's bad.' Why couldn't she remember? 'I think I'm looking for him.'

'*We are looking for him,*' Pordis corrected her.

'Yes.' Bianca got to her feet, stuffing the map back into the diary. Glimpsing the red scarf tied round her wrist again, she grasped at a hint of a memory teasing the edges of her mind. 'This is his.' She held up her hand, showing the reindeer the makeshift bracelet. 'We *are* looking for him. That's why we're here. I don't know how we arrived in this place, but we're searching for my little brother.'

'*Finn?*'

'Yes, my little brother, Finn.' Bianca put the diary back in her pocket and looked around the clearing. There appeared to be only one way out, so surely that must be the way they'd come in? But there were no footprints to suggest which direction she and Pordis had come from. Had she slept here while the snow fell? How long had they been here, in this grove?

Pordis nuzzled her nose into Bianca's side.

'What is it, Pordis?'

The reindeer shook her antlers.

'*Climb onto my back.*'

'Really?' Bianca's eyes opened wide with surprise. Did she know how to ride a reindeer? There was only one way to find out.

Pordis's toffee-coloured back was bony and about as high as a donkey's. Bianca found it easy to lift her leg over and climb on, but the reindeer's broad white neck didn't have a mane for her to cling to. Bianca lay forward, gripping the reindeer's haunches with her thighs and reached up to hold on to the antlers. 'Like this?'

'*Yes. Are you ready, my Bianca?*'

'Ready as I'll ever be,' Bianca replied, hoping she wouldn't fall off. 'Let's go find Finn.'

13

WINTERTON

Pordis trotted happily through the snow-covered forest. Staying on the reindeer's back wasn't as hard as Bianca had feared. As she relaxed, she looked around.

A reverent awe fell upon her as they travelled through the ancient trees, their branches bowed with the weight of trillions of ice crystals. Their cracked bark, the broad girth of their trunks and their soaring height led her to believe the trees were hundreds of years old, maybe thousands. From the reindeer's back she saw human and animal footprints in the snow and wondered whether one of those sets of prints belonged to her little brother.

When they emerged from the fringe of the forest,

Bianca blinked as her eyes adjusted to the dazzling landscape. They were at the top of a snowy slope that stretched down to the shore of a deep blue ocean. There were icebergs off the coast. Chunks of sea ice as big as trampolines floated about in the cove below. A pair of penguins dived from one, chasing a fish supper. Bianca closed her eyes, drawing in the fresh sea air, tasting salt on the back of her tongue. 'Oh, Pordis!' she exclaimed, blinking them open. 'This place is heavenly!'

'Yes,' Pordis agreed. *I belong here.*'

Bianca found she was smiling. Her soul felt as light as the black-capped Arctic tern she spotted scything through the sky with fanned-out tail streamers. The snowy slope was as untouched as a blank page. Bianca resisted the delightful urge to slide off Pordis's back and roll down it. 'Look! There!' Further along the shore, Bianca could see a chain of twinkling lights decorating a path that started in a cove and disappeared up through snow-capped rocks. 'I think we need to go that way.' She felt a spark of excitement. 'How do we get there.'

'*I'll find a way. Hold on tight!*' And suddenly Pordis was running, her long pink tongue hanging out of her mouth, black nose held high, head moving left then right, as they flew down the hill together.

Bianca clutched Pordis's antlers tightly, sucking in her breath as they raced towards the cliff edge. Pordis turned, galloping along the clifftop, putting on a burst of speed, her hooves kicking up snow. Bianca's hair flew back from her face, and she released her breath with an exhilarating 'WHOOP!'

Reindeer and girl cantered along the coast together, slowing as the land dropped down towards the sea and became rocky. Their path was full of twists and turns, and Bianca marvelled at Pordis's sure-footed skill.

'You're like a big, beautiful goat with antlers,' she declared happily.

Pordis stopped abruptly. *'And you are like a big, bald monkey!'* she retorted tartly.

'Oh! I'm sorry.' Bianca suppressed a giggle at the reindeer's indignant head shake. 'I didn't mean to offend you, Pordis.'

'I am a magnificent caribou, a regal reindeer. I did my best and fastest running, and for what? To be likened to a goat! Is a goat magnificent?'

Bianca tried to contain her giggle, but it exploded out of her nose with a snort, which was quickly followed by laughter. The next thing she knew, she was landing sideways in a snowdrift, having been shrugged from Pordis's back.

'Oh, Pordis, I am sorry,' Bianca said, getting up and

dusting herself off as the reindeer trotted away towards the cove with her nose in the air. 'I am a silly old bald monkey and you are magnificent. Please forgive me.'

Pordis stopped walking. *'Bianca, there is a boy by the sea.'*

Bianca ran to the reindeer's side. She saw a boy in maroon pyjamas, sitting cross-legged on a rock at the tide's edge, looking out to sea. 'Casper!' she said, finding she knew his name.

The boy turned his head and, seeing her, looked puzzled.

'It's me, Bianca,' she said, scrambling over the rocks towards him.

'Bianca . . .' Casper repeated, getting to his feet to

greet her politely. There was no flicker of recognition in his eyes.

'Hi.' She blushed, suddenly feeling shy. The orange book in her pocket said she had been to this boy's house, but all her brain could offer her was a will-o'-the-wisp memory of Casper's kind brown eyes and generous smile.

'What are you doing here all alone?'

'Oh, I'm not alone,' Casper replied. 'And people keep arriving. Like you did just now.'

Bianca wished she could remember where she knew this boy from. His cheerful voice and open manner were so familiar. 'How long have you been here?'

'I'm not sure. Not long,' he replied with a shrug. 'But maybe . . . always. What about you?'

'Yes. Same. Not long. I think.' Uneasiness fluttered in Bianca's chest like a shadow moth. Why couldn't she remember? 'I'm trying to find my brother, Finn. He's five and looks a bit like me, except with blond hair and blue eyes. Have you seen him?'

'No,' Casper replied, turning away as something out to sea drew his eye. 'Two other girls have come through here, and a boy with dark hair.'

'Why are you wearing pyjamas?' Bianca asked.

'Why aren't you?' Casper countered with a grin. 'The others were. I think it's what we wear here.'

'Do you remember where you were before you came here?'

'No.' Casper shrugged, looking back out to sea. 'But I think this place is all that matters.'

'Well, if you see my brother, can you tell him I've gone that way?' She pointed to the path.

'Mmm-hm.' Casper nodded, his eyes still fixed on the waves.

'What are you looking at?' Bianca asked, stepping onto the rock beside him.

'Monodon.' Casper pointed, and Bianca saw that there was a pod of whales swimming in the bay. One of them had a long tusk protruding from its head. 'He was waiting for me when I arrived. He took me on his back. We swam right out of the cove.'

'You rode a narwhal?' Bianca was amazed.

'If you go out far enough, you can see round that fortress on the glacier.'

In the distance, Bianca saw a glacial promontory with a towering castle of ice perched on it like an albino vulture, its translucent claws gripping the cliff edge.

'I think we're on an ice shelf,' Casper said.

'Floating out to sea?' asked Bianca.

'Yes.' A glazed look came over Casper's face.

'Is Monodon talking to you?' Bianca asked, suddenly

realizing why he was behaving strangely.

Casper's eyes flickered back to hers and he nodded.

'Pordis talks to me too.' Bianca looked over her shoulder and smiled at the reindeer. 'She's cross with me, though, because I said she was like a big goat. I meant that she was agile . . .'

Pordis huffed and lifted her nose in the air. *'Bald monkey!'*

Casper laughed. 'Monodon says I can go and play with the other children, but I'd rather stay here with the whales. They're much more fun than fairground rides.'

'Fairground rides?'

Casper nodded to the path. 'Up there. That's the way all the others went.'

'I think we have to go that way too.' She looked at the sulking reindeer. 'Come on, Pordis.'

'I hope you find your brother,' Casper said. 'If I see him, I'll say you're searching for him.'

'Thank you. His name is Finn.'

Pordis walked by Bianca's side up the track through the rocks. Overhead, vines of twinkling lights were strung in zigzags. At the path's end, suspended between two skinny fir trees, was a glittering sign in giant swirling letters of ice that said WINTERTON.

'What is this place?' Bianca whispered in wonder.

Rising before her was a huge Ferris wheel shaped like a giant snowflake. A blue neon sign proclaimed it to be the Flurry Flake. She saw a helter-skelter carved from ice and a waltzer with pretty glass carriages. Beyond the funfair, mountains emerged from the snowy plain on which Winterton was built.

Tinkling music played softly as she and Pordis strolled through the fairground. 'All the rides are empty.' Bianca peered about. 'Where is everybody?' A heavenly smell turned her head. In the centre of a square of food stalls was a fountain bubbling with steaming hot chocolate. Hanging around the rim of the fountain was a rainbow of colourful tin mugs.

'Oh! I'm starving. Come on, Pordis. Let's have a mug of hot chocolate.' She skipped over, excited to try the fountain. At its four corners were enormous white planters containing what she thought were decorative trees. She inspected the strange squishy pink fruit that were hanging from their delicate clear branches. 'Marshmallows!' she declared with delight.

Plucking one, she nibbled it cautiously, before putting the whole thing into her mouth and savouring the sweet taste. 'Delicious!' She picked three more, dropping them into a purple tin mug, which she held out under the stream of frothing hot chocolate. 'I can't have been here before,' Bianca said to Pordis, sighing contentedly as she drank deeply. 'I'd definitely remember this.' She perched on the edge of the fountain and refilled her cup.

On the far side of the square was a frozen-fruit stand with a sign saying HELP YOURSELF. Gulping down her drink, Bianca went over and picked up an empty punnet, filling it with frozen strawberries and raspberries. She beamed at Pordis. 'I wonder what else is here.' She popped a handful of tangy berries into her mouth. 'Let's explore.'

Arranged beneath giant toadstools, the size of caravans, were cosy rugs scattered with cushions. Red paper lanterns sat on mushroom tables, making the snow around them glow pink.

'Oh, look, Pordis! Up there. Someone is on that slope. They're skiing!'

A figure in a green nightshirt and shorts zoomed down the hill, long honey-coloured hair flying behind her. When she reached the bottom, the girl leaned to one side, turning, carving the snow in a semicircle with the blades of her skis, till she came to a neat stop.

'I know her, Pordis!' Bianca exclaimed, running towards the girl and waving. 'That's Sophie!' Pordis trotted by her side, but they both stopped suddenly when they saw a large cat bounding down the slope, its huge paws barely leaving a print on the snow. It

had silver fur, leopard-like spots and a long, bushy tail. For one terrible moment, Bianca thought the cat was going to pounce on Sophie and eat her, but instead it rubbed its head affectionately against her side and Sophie scratched behind its ears.

'Sophie, it's me, Bianca!' she called out as they got closer.

'Hi,' Sophie called back, looking at her with no sign of recognition. 'Do you want to come up the slopes and ski with us? The powder is as fresh and fluffy as eiderdown stuffing.'

'Er . . .' Bianca stared at the cat, who glowered back with unblinking eyes. 'No thanks.'

'Oh, don't mind Lumi,' Sophie added. 'She's a friendly snow leopard. Aren't you, Lumi?' She tickled the big cat's chin. 'Come on. It's brilliant up there. When you're at the top, you can see right across Winterton.'

'Oh, all right,' Bianca said, walking forward, but then she stopped and frowned. 'Hang on. No. I can't. There's something I've got to do first. Er, what was it?' She scratched her head and spotted the little red scarf around her wrist. 'Oh! I've got to find my brother!'

'Have you lost him?'

'I . . . I must have.' Bianca felt a jolt of alarm that she had forgotten Finn in the short time it had taken her to get from Casper to Sophie.

'Well, I can see all the children arriving from up there.' Sophie pointed up the slope. 'I saw you and your reindeer come out of the forest.'

'Is everyone here a child?' Bianca asked, feeling uneasy. She couldn't put her finger on it, but there was something about the wonderful Winterton that didn't feel right.

'Yes. Isn't it great?' Sophie unclipped her skis. 'Right, we're going back up.' She climbed onto Lumi's back. 'What's your brother's name?'

'Finn. He's five. If you see him, tell him I'm in the fairground, looking for him.'

'Got it,' Sophie said as the snow leopard padded away. 'See you later!'

Bianca watched the big cat bound up the mountain.

'You wouldn't dare call Lumi a big goat,' said Pordis.

14

HUNTED

Children of all ages were arriving in Winterton, in groups of increasing size, and each child came with an animal companion. Opposite the fairground, on a flat white tundra, two teams were enthusiastically crafting snowballs and stacking them in piles.

'You just wait,' one excited girl in polka-dot pyjamas shouted. 'You're going to be obliterated.'

'Oh yeah? We're going to take you down,' came a reply.

'Prepare for utter annihilation!' someone squealed.

'You'll be eating snow for breakfast, lunch and dinner!' a boy howled in delight.

A snowy owl lifted one of the snowballs, flew across the battlefield and dropped it on the head of an opposing team player. Everyone fell about laughing. The boy splattered with snow grabbed a snowball, hurled it, and the fight began. The shrieks and whoops of laughter made Bianca long to join in. But she gripped the tiny red scarf tied around her wrist. She mustn't be distracted from the reason she'd come to Winterton.

This place makes people forget, she thought, and looked down at the half-eaten punnet of frozen fruit she held in her hand. Had the berries, or the hot chocolate, made her forgetful? She looked for a place to set the punnet down. She couldn't risk eating or drinking any more of the food here.

As she and Pordis searched Winterton for Finn, Bianca couldn't help feeling that she was somehow different from the rest of the children. They were living in the moment, unconcerned with anything except enjoying what they were doing. Shrieks of delight and laughter erupted from a group as their giant snowball rolled away from them. They were building a snowman and called out for her to join them. She smiled and shook her head.

'Pordis, the children in Winterton are not like me.'

'Is it because they do not have a brother to find?'

'Perhaps.' Bianca wondered why she wasn't wearing nightclothes when everyone else was.

They came to a frozen lake where a small girl with short, dark hair was skating across the ice in a billowing blue nightie, moving in hypnotic loops. She held her arms behind her, arched like the wings of a swan. Her dance partner was a baby polar bear. It looked at her adoringly, skating in circles around her, sliding on its bottom when it needed to slow down.

For some reason Bianca felt relieved to see this girl and she found she knew her name. 'Gwen!'

Seeing Bianca, the girl pirouetted, then skated over, the baby polar bear by her side.

'Hello!' Gwen greeted her, breathless and smiling.

'It's good to see you,' Bianca said, not knowing why this was true.

'Sorry.' Gwen looked puzzled. 'Do I know you?'

'I'm Bianca.'

'Hello, Bianca. You can get ice skates over there, from the funny birds.' Gwen pointed to an igloo beside the lake. It had an open front with a counter. On the counter was a pile of fish, silver herrings. Two puffins with white breasts, black backs and bright orange webbed feet were hopping around it, getting in each other's way as they ate the fish. Behind them, lined up on shelves, were pairs of white leather skates with silver blades. The larger bird saw that Bianca was looking at them. It opened its beak wide in a smile, dropping its fish, and pointed a wing at the skates, hopping up and down excitedly. 'Are you going to skate with us?' Gwen asked.

'I can't.' Bianca turned back to the girl. 'I'm looking for Finn, my brother. He's your age. I was wondering if you'd seen him?'

'No. Grendel and I have been dancing on the ice since we got here. I haven't seen anyone.'

'Well, if you do see him, can you say that I'm looking for him?'

'Do I know him?' Gwen looked confused.

'I think so,' Bianca replied uncertainly.

'Oh, OK,' Gwen said, skating backwards, away from her. 'If I see a Finn, I'll say you're looking for him.'

'*Bianca!*' Pordis's voice rushed into her head.

'What is it?' Bianca sensed fear in the reindeer.

'*We must hide!*'

'Hide?'

'*Quick!*'

The reindeer cantered to the igloo where the puffins were playing tug of war with a fish. Bianca sprinted after her.

'Hello,' she said to the squabbling birds. 'Mind if we duck behind here for a second?'

Without letting go of their fish, the birds nodded their orange beaks up and down.

Bianca slid over the counter, dropping into a squat as Pordis nimbly bounded over and knelt down beside her. 'Who are we hiding from?' Bianca whispered to Pordis as one of the puffins hopped onto a branch of the reindeer's antlers, which poked up above the worktop.

'*A bear!*'

Bianca was about to protest that they needn't be

afraid of bears here when she heard a voice that made her gasp.

'I didn't mean to smash the windows,' came a booming grumble. 'It was an accident. I got excited.'

Bianca recognized the voice, and knew in the marrow of her bones that she feared the person it belonged to. Risking a peek over the counter, she saw three children: a boy in a bearskin, and twins, a brother and sister, dressed in grey. Ducking back down, she pulled her orange diary from her pocket, flicking to the drawings she'd done of four children. It was them! Three of them, at least: Quilo, Pitter and Patter. Was the drawing a warning?

'Jack says it attracted attention . . .' Pitter said.

'. . . and we don't have to mention . . .' Patter added.

'. . . that a silver book has gone.' Pitter sounded fearful.

'He feels that something's wrong . . .' Patter whined.

'. . . in our wondrous Winterton,' Pitter concluded.

'Why is it only what Jack feels that matters?' Quilo protested sulkily.

'We don't wish to be unkind . . .' Patter sounded insincere.

'. . . but it was you who left the book behind,' Pitter said accusingly.

'And Jack precedes *her*,' Pitter told Quilo.

'Jack's our leader!' Patter agreed.

Bianca risked another peep over the counter.

'I drive the queen's carriage, and I think I'd be a pretty good leader if I was given half a—' The boy in the bear suit didn't finish because the twins were laughing at him. He folded his arms across his chest and harrumphed. 'If it was that Bianca girl who stole our book, we'll find her. All we have to do is keep looking.' He pointed to Gwen on the frozen lake. 'Look, there's a girl.'

The twins pivoted to see, then sprinted towards the lake. In unison, they leaped unfeasibly high into the air, their grey shoes growing icy blades before they landed on the ice. Skating hard, they built up speed, somersaulting and twirling around Gwen and the baby polar bear.

Bianca watched them stop Gwen and talk to her. She saw Gwen nod and point towards the fairground.

'Silly girl,' Bianca whispered. But she hadn't asked Gwen not to tell anyone that she'd seen her. Bianca hadn't realized she should be hiding. She was going to have to be more careful from now on.

Pitter and Patter raced back to Quilo, gabbling as they finished each other's sentences.

'Bianca Albedo! She was here.'

'Her winter creature's a female reindeer.'

'Gwen says she's looking for her brother . . .'

'. . . dressed in day clothes of a purple colour!'

'Well, good,' Quilo burped. 'That will make her easy to spot.'

'She mustn't find the boy.' Pitter sounded worried.

'He's the queen's favourite toy!' Patter nodded.

Bianca held her breath as she heard this.

'Then let's hurry. If she was just here, we'll catch up with her easily. Then we can throw her in the palace dungeons until the winter solstice is over. That should calm things down. Jack says she could ruin our scheme, but I say that's piffle. She's just a girl.'

'She could,' Pitter warned.

'It's not good.' Patter shook her head.

'Is it really that bad? I know Jack says we can't have siblings here, that the blood bond between them is too strong and will attract memories, but she must have read *The Vanishing World*. Her heart will have been pierced by the splinter. It will be freezing, like all the others.' Quilo waved an arm, gesturing to the children playing in the distance. 'When the winter solstice arrives, all their hearts will be turned to ice, including hers.' He marched away. 'You'll see.'

'Catch her we must . . .' muttered Patter.

'. . . or lose Jack's trust,' agreed Pitter, and they hurried after him.

136

Bianca clutched her right hand to her chest in terror. Her heart had been pierced by a splinter! She felt the reassuring throb of her pulse beneath her skin. How could her heart be freezing if she could feel it beating? Could she trust her body, or was it her mind playing tricks? She realized with a jolt that she hadn't felt the cold at all since she'd arrived, even though she was surrounded by ice and snow.

'*Bianca,*' Pordis whispered inside her head, nudging her wet nose against Bianca's neck. '*Are you all right, my Bianca?*'

'Pordis,' she whispered softly. 'Those children – Quilo, Pitter and Patter, and the one they called Jack – they took my brother from me. They've done something to me and all the children here. I think we're dying!' Fear and anger fought to rule her head. She gritted her teeth, trying to conquer them both with her mind. 'I made it here, even though they didn't want me to. And they say I have the power to ruin their plan, whatever that is.'

'*We will find Finn,*' Pordis said.

'Yes.' Bianca looked deep into the reindeer's brown eyes. 'And we must be getting close, or they wouldn't be so worried.'

15

FLURRY FLAKE

'hat are we going to do? They're looking for a girl in purple clothes with a reindeer.' Bianca looked down at her jumper and her open coat in despair. 'We'll be caught immediately.' She felt panicky. 'We need a disguise.'

'*What is a disguise?*' Pordis tilted her head.

'We need to make you look like something else. Something that isn't a reindeer.' Bianca looked hard at Pordis's antlers. They were going to be difficult to hide.

'*I can walk on my hind legs like a human.*'

'You can?'

'*Yes,*' Pordis said proudly. '*I can do seven steps before I fall over.*'

'Hmm, I don't think that's going to work.' Bianca got to her feet, fastening her coat to hide her purple jumper. 'Wait here. I'll be back as soon as I can.'

Running to the spot where she had seen the snowman being built, Bianca called out to the children, 'Can I help?'

'We're making a snowman parade,' a tall boy replied, nodding eagerly, and pointed at five towers of snow. The snowman he was working on was wearing a yellow dressing gown.

'Brilliant,' Bianca said, grabbing a handful of snow and patting it into a gap on the nearest snowman's body. 'What are you going to dress the others in?'

'Don't know,' he admitted with a shrug, and she guessed the dressing gown had been his.

'There are loads of rugs and stuff over there.' She pointed to the giant toadstools.

'Ooh, that's a good idea,' said a girl in pink pyjamas who was rolling a ball of snow with a friend. 'Come on.' And the pair raced away.

The tall boy loped after them. 'Wait for me!'

Moving fast, Bianca took out her diary and peeled off her coat. As she hurriedly swapped it for the yellow dressing gown, she knocked the two branches that were the snowman's arms onto the ground. They gave her an idea. She put on the yellow dressing gown, slipped her diary into a pocket and, flipping up the collar, she crossed the gown over her front and tied the belt, hiding her purple jumper. She kicked snow over the two branches on the ground, covering them up.

When the others came back with arms full of fabric, she grabbed a sparkling sheet, threaded with silver, and a fluffy white blanket. She pretended to dress her snowman, but when the others were busy she grabbed the branches, turned and ran.

On reaching the igloo, Bianca called for Pordis to come out.

'We're going to pretend,' Bianca said, throwing the fluffy blanket over Pordis's back so that it hung down on either side and hid her legs, 'that you are a snow pony who desperately wants to be a reindeer.'

'*But I am a reindeer!*'

'I know, but they're not looking for a girl in a yellow dressing gown with a silly snow pony.' Bianca grabbed an ice skate and slashed at the sparkling sheet, ripping it into ribbons. 'I'll make fake antlers with the branches and a tail like a pony's out of these ribbons.' She knotted the ribbons, tying them together. 'I'm going to make a hat from the branches and strap it to your real antlers. Hopefully it will make them look fake.'

'*And this is a good disguise?*' Pordis asked, looking perplexed.

'No.' Bianca laughed. 'It's terrible, but you're a difficult creature to conceal, unless we saw off your antlers.'

'*Don't you dare!*'

'Silly snow pony it is, then!'

It was a very strange reindeer that shuffled away from the igloo. Bianca thanked the puffins and led Pordis towards the fairground by her homemade bridle.

'Sway a little from side to side with each step,' Bianca whispered. 'Try not to be so graceful. Snow ponies lumber a bit more on account of their stubby legs, or at least Shetland ponies do, and I think they're nearly the same.'

A grinning boy with a white hawk on his arm pointed at Pordis. 'What kind of creature is that?'

'This is a reindeer,' Bianca answered, then behind her hand whispered loudly. 'She's a snow pony, but she wants to be a reindeer, so I made her antlers.'

'Hello, Mrs Reindeer,' the boy greeted Pordis with a laugh. 'Nice antlers you've got there.'

To Bianca's surprise, Pordis snorted air through her nose and made a whinnying sound just like a horse.

The boy winked at Bianca as she carried on, and

after a minute she heard him telling another child about the snow pony that thought it was a reindeer.

'Pordis, that was brilliant,' Bianca muttered.

'*Oh yes, I am very adaptable. I can be a goat, a pony, even a reindeer!*'

Bianca chuckled, turning as she heard the sort of twinkling music that might accompany a troupe of dancing imps. It was coming from the Flurry Flake Ferris wheel. As they drew nearer, it occurred to her that from up there she'd be able to see the whole of Winterton.

'Pordis, we're going to take a ride on the big wheel.'

'*Must we?*' Pordis sounded less than enthusiastic. '*I'm not a bird.*'

'I want to see Winterton from up there,' Bianca replied. 'Once we're in the carriage and the wheel is turning, we'll be safe from discovery for a bit.'

'*All right,*' Pordis grumbled. '*Perhaps I'll be able to take this blanket off for a little while. You've no idea how hot it is under here.*'

When the Flurry Flake came to a stop, Bianca steered Pordis to join the queue.

The carriage Bianca and Pordis stepped into was a giant glass bauble etched with stars. Inside, the floor and seat were covered in plush white velvet.

As the car rose, Bianca felt the weight of fear lifting

from her shoulders. They were safe in here while the wheel turned. She stared out across Winterton, and when they reached the top she moved in her seat to gaze at the ice fortress. She couldn't see any windows. It looked like a cluster of giant stalagmites. She wondered what kind of queen lived in a place like that.

What had Pitter and Patter said? *'She mustn't find the boy . . . He's the queen's favourite toy.'* She felt certain they'd been talking about Finn. But who was this Queen of Winterton?

She imagined how cold and severe the dungeons would be in a fortress like that, deep within the glacier. She desperately hoped Finn wasn't in there, and wished she could recall how he'd been taken. Her mind was full of blanks, snowdrifts covering up memories.

Pulling her diary from the dressing-gown pocket, she flicked through it, page by page, realizing she wasn't even certain what day it was today.

An entry on the page for the first of December caught her eye: FINN FROZEN. What did that mean? She read some notes about a silver book. They made no sense to her, although she remembered that the grey twins had accused Quilo of leaving a book behind. Had she taken it? She couldn't remember.

On the second of December, she had written SOPHIE & CASPER FROZEN. But she had seen both Sophie and Casper today and they were fine.

'It's a puzzle,' Bianca muttered to herself, looking out at the children playing in Winterton as the carriage descended. More and more of them seemed to be arriving all the time. Did they all have splinters in their hearts? She now saw the town for what it was: a dazzling distraction, a magician's trick. The rides and games were designed to keep children playing while their hearts slowly froze.

For the first time since she'd woken up here, Bianca truly felt the peril of this strange, snowy land. As the wheel turned, she looked down at the laughing girls and boys, eating ice cream and frozen yogurt below her. A train of sledges pulled by teams of huskies was setting off. The sledges were full of grinning passengers. None of them knew the danger they were in.

'I don't like it here,' she said eventually.

'*Yes,*' Pordis agreed. '*If reindeers were meant to go up into the sky, we'd have wings.*'

'Not on the wheel! I mean Winterton.' Bianca smiled at Pordis. 'But I think the ride is coming to an end now.'

'*Finally!*' Pordis exclaimed, getting to her feet.

When the Flurry Flake halted, they climbed from

the carriage and Bianca heard a jaunty tune being played on a flute, accompanied by delicate chimes. In her diary, it said that she was having flute lessons. 'Where's that music coming from?' she wondered, looking around.

'*Over there.*' Pordis pointed with her antlers.

The Winterton children were crowding towards a large white marquee. Boys and girls, and their companion creatures, flooded through the open side of the tent.

'Let's join the crowd,' Bianca said to Pordis. 'There's safety in numbers. When we get inside, we'll find a spot in the middle of the audience.'

The floor of the tent was covered in sheepskin rugs and the walls were decorated with floaty drapes. At the far end, on a raised platform, was a band of musicians.

At the back of the stage a walrus was using his blubbery body as a percussive instrument, slapping and beating time with his flippers. Beside him, a dopey-looking musk ox was emitting a hypnotic bass hum, which rose and fell to a melody an Arctic fox played on a silver flute. The fox was flanked by a pair of biscuit-white seals blowing into pan pipes using their nostrils. At the front, an Arctic ermine ran backwards and forwards, plucking on the strings of a harp. A string of icicles hung along the top of the stage and, perched above them, was a snowy owl, which bobbed her head, hooted and then pecked a couple of icicles, making them chime delicately. The star turn of the band was a giant polar bear sitting on his haunches in the middle of the stage, rubbing the wet pads of his paws round the rims of ice bowls containing different amounts of water. The music was strange and hypnotic.

'It's a show!' Bianca whispered to Pordis as they sat down in the middle of a group of children. 'Do you think Finn is here?' She scanned the faces of the children pouring into the tent. There were so many of them, hundreds it seemed.

As the mesmerizing music built to a climax, a troupe of six penguins slid onto the stage on their bellies. They leaped to their webbed feet, with their flippers held up high. The audience of children applauded.

A hush fell as the penguins danced, dipping their heads to the music, weaving between one another in a reel, lifting their feet one way then the other. One of the penguins, the third in line, got distracted and waved a flipper at them, falling out of time. The children beside Bianca giggled and waved back.

The musk ox bellowed out a low trumpeting sound and the walrus beat his flippers against his chest in a

drumroll. A seventh penguin was lowered from above the stage on strings, swinging above the heads of the six dancers, looking self-important as he pretended to fly.

Bianca smiled, despite herself. Lots of children were laughing.

The out-of-time penguin was distracted by the laughter and trod on the foot of the bird next to him, who fell over.

Bianca chuckled, glancing across the clapping, cheering audience, hoping she might spy her brother's toothless grin, and suddenly her heart clenched.

The grey twins were walking through the audience, checking the children and their creatures. They were looking for her. She knew it. But if she and Pordis got up and moved they'd be seen.

She was trapped.

16

SNOW HAVEN

'**P**ordis,' Bianca gasped. 'They're going to find us!'
'*What shall we do?*'

'I don't know!' Bianca looked about in alarm. 'We're going to have to split up. You creep to the back of the tent. I'll edge towards the side. Stay low. Try and find a moment when you can dodge out of the door without being seen, then run as fast as you can. I'll do the same, but I'll slip out the side, under the tent flaps.'

'*I won't leave you,*' Pordis said. '*You're my herd.*'

Bianca leaned her forehead against Pordis's long snout. 'You're my herd too,' she whispered. 'But you must do as I say. When the coast is clear, we'll meet down in the cove, where we saw Casper. OK?'

'Yes, my Bianca,' Pordis replied, as Bianca hurriedly untied the branches she'd strapped to the reindeer's antlers.

The penguins cleared the stage, getting ready for the next act, and the audience grew impatient, wriggling and chattering.

'Go, go, go!' Bianca hissed, removing the blanket and fake tail.

As Pordis retreated, Bianca sneaked forward.

The audience fell silent as a small grizzly bear lumbered onto the stage on all fours. From the opposite wings, a pale willow-thin figure in a white suit and black top hat strode forward.

Bianca's whole body stiffened in shock. It was Jack!

The pale figure bowed, removing the top hat. Reaching into it with a gloved hand, the white-eyed magician pulled out a long ivory silk scarf, tossing it high into the air. As it reached the apex of its flight, the scarf divided into a hundred tiny fluttering butterflies.

The grizzly bear sat back on its haunches, puffing little eddying breaths at the silk butterflies, sending them whirling upwards, as the Arctic orchestra played a puckish tune.

The audience cooed, but Bianca was transfixed with fear.

Jack's eyes glittered, looking everywhere and nowhere at once.

Bianca didn't dare move. She couldn't tell if she'd been seen or not.

Jack took off the white gloves, revealing giant snowflake hands, and an image flashed into Bianca's mind of Jack standing by a big machine, ice spooling from those unnatural fingers, making silver books.

I remember! Bianca thought, fixing the image in her mind. *I remember the books!*

The grizzly bear threw back its head, revealing the rosy-cheeked face of Quilo.

The audience clapped and cheered.

Bianca screwed her eyes tightly shut, and focused her entire mind into two words. *'RUN, PORDIS!'* she shouted, silently, inside her own head.

Hearing Pordis grunt, Bianca looked over her shoulder and saw the reindeer cantering away from the tent.

Quick as a flash, Pitter and Patter were sprinting after her. Bianca shuffled sideways, trapped between children, unable to run.

One of Jack's strange hands waved in a graceful arc, making a frost fern grow in the air before them. The tune from the orchestra sank into a minor key as Quilo took a deep breath and puffed a ball of wind at the glistening plant, shattering it into shards. The wind created a vortex in which the crystals spun, and the music built, as if this had all been rehearsed.

Jack slowly turned, smiling right at Bianca, breaking her free of the trance created by his ice-conjuring.

Fear flared inside her chest, and Bianca bolted for the nearest side of the tent. Hearing Quilo's roar, she glanced back and saw the ice shards, like stiletto knives, flying towards her back.

Throwing herself to the ground, Bianca rolled out of the tent, wrenching out pegs.

Stumbling to her feet, she ran blindly away from the marquee, certain that Jack and Quilo were right behind her.

She was shocked to find that Winterton was empty. All the children and animals were inside the theatre tent.

They lured us in with the music, Bianca realized as she ran. *Was the show just a trap for me?*

If all the children in Winterton were inside the marquee, and she hadn't seen Finn, then Bianca knew, with a soul-darkening dread, that there was only one place left that her brother could be: inside the ice fortress.

She ducked down behind a coconut shy with sculpted ice targets and snowball ammunition.

Running bent double, she made it to the helter-skelter, risking a glance over her shoulder as she rounded the cylindrical slide. She didn't see anyone following her, but she knew they couldn't be far away. Her breath was coming in short gasps and her throat burned.

Darting away from the slide, she made it to the base of the Flurry Flake, pausing for breath as she hid behind the wheel's drive mechanism. Then Bianca put on a burst of speed, sprinting under the WINTERTON sign and down the rocky path back to the sea.

Hurtling down the track at a breakneck pace, Bianca burst out onto the beach, desperately searching the shore for Pordis. She spotted Casper, still sitting on his rock beside the sea, watching the whales.

'Casper!' she panted as she stumbled over to him. 'I need your help.'

'What is it?' Casper sprang to his feet.

'There are people trying to stop me from finding my brother.' Bianca bent over, leaning on her knees, gulping down air. 'They tried to trap me. I ran. I don't know where Pordis went.'

'Did you find Finn?'

Bianca shook her head. 'He's not in Winterton.'

'Where is he?'

Bianca pointed to the far-off fortress, and Casper's eyes grew wide.

'Pordis!' Bianca cried, as the reindeer finally appeared on the beach.

'*My Bianca!*'

Pordis raced towards her, and Bianca fell to her knees in front of her companion, wrapping her arms round her neck and rubbing her forehead against the reindeer's long snout.

'Are you all right, my Pordis?'

'*The boy and the girl chased me across the field of snow. Then, suddenly, they stopped and turned back.*'

'Clever Pordis. They must've known they'd never catch you,' Bianca said, getting to her feet. 'Did you see anyone near the path when you came down to the cove?'

'*No one.*'

'Monodon says you shouldn't go to the palace,' Casper said. 'He says it's dangerous. There's something terrible in Snow Haven. Something dying.'

'Snow Haven?'

'That's what the fortress is called.'

'I don't care if there's a deadly monster inside.' Bianca put her hands on her hips and glared out to sea. 'If Finn is in there, then I'm going in too.'

'The path to the palace is long and dangerous.' Casper pointed up at the rocky cliff. 'You'll have to go back through Winterton and out that way.'

156

Bianca's heart sank as she looked at the path, which was exposed on all sides. She would be seen approaching the fortress. Even if she could get there, she'd be caught. Her hand went to her heart as she glanced at the sky. The light hadn't changed since she'd woken up here. How long had it been since she'd arrived? It felt like forever and no time at all. Surely the sun should be setting? Her sense of unease grew as she cast around for a plan. She didn't know how much time she had.

Casper's eyes glazed over, then he blinked. 'There is another way. Monodon and I can take you.'

'How?' Bianca looked out to sea, and swallowed. 'I don't think I can ride a whale.'

Pordis grunted. '*I certainly can't!*'

'You don't have to. Though you don't know what you're missing.' Casper pointed at a slab of sea ice coming towards them.

Beyond it, Bianca saw the unique counter-clockwise spiralling horn of the narwhal that earned it the nickname, 'unicorn of the sea'. The whale was black, speckled white, with a powerful tail, small fins and friendly dark eyes.

'Monodon suggests we climb aboard the ice, and he'll push us. There's a landing place, where the penguins fish, at the foot of the cliff.'

'Us?'

'You don't think I'd send you off on an adventure with Monodon on your own, do you?' Casper grinned, jumping onto the ice raft. 'Anyway, it sounds like you need all the help you can get.'

'Oh, thank you!' Bianca immediately felt stronger with Casper's support.

'*You're not leaving me behind*,' Pordis said, walking onto the ice craft and sitting down.

Bianca smiled and stepped aboard. 'And thank you, Monodon.' She knelt down, looking at the whale in the water. 'I won't forget this. You and Casper are both good friends to help us.'

Swimming under their raft of ice, Monodon propelled the strange sea vessel out of the bay. The intimidatingly pale, spiky fortress was set against the vivid blue sky. As they drew closer, it began to dawn on Bianca  how enormous Snow Haven actually was.

How was she going to find her little brother in there? And what was the dangerous creature dying inside?

17

SNOW GOLEMS

As their ice raft got closer and closer, the fortress grew in stature and menace, making Bianca feel very small. The building's foundations appeared to spring from the rocks and the ice. It didn't look like a man-made structure.

Casper pointed to a natural jetty, a rocky spur far below the fortress. 'That's where we'll land.'

Monodon was heading straight towards it. When they were close, the narwhal kicked his tail fin and the front of the ice raft lifted, beaching on the rock.

Bianca craned her neck, studying the route up to the castle. They'd have to pass along an icy ledge to a narrow path through the rocks that led to the snowy hill on which Snow Haven sat. 'I can do this,' she whispered to herself, and jumped off the raft, scrambling over the rocks to the ledge. Pordis followed her.

'Casper, you don't have to come,' Bianca said as he leaped off the ice raft too.

'I know,' Casper replied, glancing up at the looming fortress, 'but I can't watch you go in there alone.'

Bianca smiled at him gratefully.

'We'll be back as soon as we can,' Casper said to Monodon, and the narwhal blew a jet of water into the air through his blowhole. 'Don't worry. We'll be careful.'

Climbing up the snowy ledge towards the base of the castle was hard going. They progressed in silence until they reached a gap in the cliff where a narrow path stretched beneath an overhanging crust of snow. Icicles, like translucent tigers' teeth, hung precariously above their heads. Bianca and Casper crept along holding their breath, lest their movement loosen the icy darts.

In Winterton, there had been music and laughter, but out here all Bianca could hear was the whistling wind and crashing waves.

When they finally reached the base of the snowy slope up to the fortress, Bianca got down on all fours to climb it. A strong wind pushed against her, so that she kept sliding back down. Casper tried, and met the same fate. If she hadn't known better, Bianca would have thought the wind was working against them, pushing them down on purpose.

'*Get behind me and hold on,*' Pordis said.

The reindeer was surer footed in the snow and less affected by the wind. Bianca and Casper each had a hand on the reindeer's back as they struggled up the snowy slope.

As they climbed higher, Bianca felt the wind getting stronger, but she refused to let it beat her. She leaned closer to the ground, digging her fingers into the snow, sheltering behind Pordis's flank.

Despite the wind's best efforts, they reached the top, and to Bianca's surprise, once they were away from the edge, it died down completely.

'That was hard work,' Casper said, pausing to catch his breath.

'We made it, though,' Bianca said triumphantly, turning towards Snow Haven. The fortress had no gates. It didn't need them. Beyond a plain of snow, the entrance, an immense archway, was waiting to swallow them.

'*Something's coming,*' Pordis warned, nervously taking a step backwards.

A terrifying thunderous noise shook the earth beneath them. Bianca's knees buckled, and she fell to the ground beside Casper as two great pillars of snow rose up before them. At first, they had no recognizable form, but the shoulders grew broad and a round, helmeted head appeared on each pillar.

'*Snow golems!*' Pordis exclaimed.

'What are snow golems?' Bianca's voice came out in a frightened squeak as spears of ice grew in the creatures' hands.

'Snow golems?' Casper looked alarmed.

'*Guardians,*' Pordis said. '*Soldiers.*'

Bianca and Casper held on to one another as they got to their feet.

An eerie blue light sparked in the eyeholes of each snow golem. They levelled their weapons at Bianca's chest. '*State your business,*' came their ghoulish whisper.

Bianca swallowed and, trying to sound cheerful and light-hearted, asked, 'Are people allowed into Snow Haven to visit guests?'

The snow golems didn't answer. Nor did they stand aside or lower their weapons.

'I guess that means no,' Bianca muttered, glancing at Casper.

'We heard the palace is getting dirty,' Casper tried. 'We're the cleaners. We're here to give it a bit of a polish.'

There was no response from the snow golems.

Bianca suddenly darted forward, but they blocked her path with their spears and growled until she stepped back.

'Aaaarrrgghhhh!' Casper suddenly yelled as he

ran at one of the golems.

The golem disintegrated and Casper fell face first into the snow. The second golem pointed his ice spear at Casper and growled at him until he'd returned to Bianca's side.

The disintegrated golem re-formed in front of them.

'That was brave,' Bianca whispered.

'Thanks,' Casper replied, shaking his head and spitting out snow. 'How are we going to get past them?'

'Any ideas, Pordis?'

'I have not.'

Every one of Pordis's muscles was tensed for flight, and Bianca realized that the reindeer was scared.

'Hey,' Bianca called to the golems. 'Do you know who I am? I'm Bianca Albedo.'

'What are you doing?' Casper hissed.

Both golems' heads turned, and they fixed their glowing blue eyes on her.

'Tell Jack I'm here. Quilo, Pitter and Patter are all looking for me. They want me thrown in the Snow Haven dungeons. Casper –' she pointed at him – 'brought me here. I will end up in that castle whether you let me walk in myself, or we wait until Jack orders you to take me in.'

The golems looked at each other, and the blue light in their eyes faded for a moment, as if they were sending a message. Then it flared again.

Bianca stood before them with her chin raised and her hands on her hips. 'So, are you going to let us in or what?'

The golems bowed their heads, stepping aside. Then they disintegrated, caving in on themselves, once again becoming heaps of snow.

'That was weird,' Casper said, staring at them. 'Now I'm really nervous.'

'Me too. We no longer have the advantage of surprise,' Bianca said, clambering over the heaps of snow. 'Come on. The sooner we find Finn, the sooner we can get out of here.'

Dusting off her hands, she stared up at the icicle fortress. The building was a Gothic basilica of ice, with countless lofty towers that tapered into sharp spikes. The mottled exteriors were dimpled like white honeycomb. The walls made her think of wax dripping from melting candles.

'It's not too late to turn back,' Casper said nervously.

'It is for me,' Bianca said. 'Finn is in there. He has to be.' She wondered if she should tell Casper about his freezing heart, but knew that she couldn't. She wished she didn't know about her own.

'In we go, then,' Casper said, without moving.

'*Something inside is in pain,*' Pordis said, trotting

forward to lead the way.

The entrance was a yawning archway. On either side were columns as large in height and girth as the trees of Firfrost Forest. Pordis entered it first, the sound of her hooves echoing in the grand porch. There came a horrible grinding noise as four barred walls rose up around the reindeer and a roof dropped down, capturing her in a cage.

'Bianca!'

'Pordis!' Bianca cried, running forward. 'NO!'

There was a clanking sound as the cage lifted high into the air, suspended from the roof of the porch by a chain of ice.

'Pordis!' Bianca cried again, jumping up, but she could not reach the cage. She and Casper urgently searched about for a lever or switch that might release it, but found none.

'It was a trap!' Bianca gasped, sinking to the floor. She was trembling and on the brink of tears, but refused to cry. She needed to be brave.

'My Bianca, I am not hurt,' Pordis reassured her.

'Pordis, I don't know what to do!'

'Yes, you do. You must go on without me,' Pordis said. 'Find Finn.'

'But you are my herd,' Bianca said with her mind's voice.

'*And so is Finn,*' came the reindeer's reply.

'*I'm sorry.*' Bianca's eyes filled with tears.

'*Don't be sorry. Be brave, my Bianca.*'

Taking a deep breath, she took Casper's hand and got to her feet.

'Pordis, once I've found Finn, I'll come and get you.'

'*I know you will, my brave Bianca.*'

'Are you all right?' Casper asked, looking at her with concern.

Bianca pressed her lips together and nodded.

'We've got to be careful.' He looked around. 'Who knows what traps are waiting for us in this place.'

'Which way should we go?' Bianca wiped her eyes.

'Let's try this way,' Casper said, walking through a smaller archway into a grand lobby. The ice walls and floor inside the palace glowed with light, and the whiteness was blinding and disorientating. Smaller arches led to a labyrinth of passageways on all sides of the room.

'Which one do we take?' Bianca asked, looking around.

'Well, I guess we just pick one. Are you feeling lucky?'

Bianca shook her head.

'OK, I'll choose.' Casper peered down each of the passages in turn, finally pointing to one on his left.

'This way.' He smiled at her, then marched confidently through the archway.

Bianca moved to follow him, but Casper suddenly cried out as the ground beneath him crumbled, and he fell.

18

THE FROST GARDEN

Bianca's scream ricocheted off the walls of Snow Haven. She ran towards the place where, only moments ago, Casper had been standing. Getting down on her hands and knees, she crawled to the edge of the hole that had swallowed him. It was a chute carved from ice, twisting and turning, disappearing into the glacier.

'Casper?' she called down it, but there was no reply, only the echo of her own voice.

Where had Casper gone? Was he in the dungeons? Was the monster down there?

Bianca moved away from the hole. She leaned back against the archway, hugging her knees to her chest. This was hopeless. They'd barely got through the door of Snow Haven and already Pordis and Casper had been captured. She'd never make it to Finn on her own. She dropped her head, feeling drained of energy.

'*You must go on.*' Pordis's soft voice sounded in her head. '*Find Finn.*'

'*I can't,*' Bianca said in her mind's voice. '*I'm so tired.*'

'*They are frightened of you. Remember, they said that you could ruin their scheme, not just save Finn.*'

Ruin their scheme? Bianca lifted her head. What did that mean? She'd been so determined to find and save her brother, it hadn't occurred to her that she might have the power to stop Jack, Quilo, Pitter and Patter – whatever they were doing, or why ever they were doing it. None of the other children in Winterton had memories, only her, and she wasn't supposed to have any. All their hearts were being frozen, including hers. Could she stop that? How? She had no idea. But, if she had the power to ruin Jack's scheme, she was going to try.

Getting to her feet, Bianca steeled herself as she examined each of the archways leading off the lobby in turn. There were eight of them, and they appeared identical. She looked back along the passageway that had swallowed Casper.

'If I were putting traps in passageways,' Bianca

muttered to herself, 'I'd put one in the passageway that led somewhere important.'

Taking a few steps back, Bianca ran at the passageway and leaped over the hole that held the chute. Landing firmly on the other side, exhaling with relief, she crept forward carefully, testing the ground with each step. It was solid here. She continued towards an open door in the base of a tall tower. She poked her head through and looked up.

'That is a lot of steps!' she whispered to herself as her eyes followed the ever-spiralling staircase upwards. Something moved near her face. Jerking back in alarm, Bianca saw a translucent turquoise dragonfly flit past and rise up the stairwell.

Where did you come from? she wondered, turning around and studying the walls around her. There were no other doors or turnings. She stood in the middle of the corridor, reached out her arms so that they were touching both ice walls, then retraced her steps. Two metres back, the wall on her left stopped. There was an opening she had missed because everything was so dazzlingly white.

Holding her arms out in front of her, Bianca felt her way through the opening and came up against a wall. She turned, feeling her way around it, and drew in a surprised gasp as she found herself in a breathtakingly beautiful bower of ice flowers. In front of her stretched a path through a courtyard garden, the like of which she'd never imagined. Her eyes hungrily devoured every delicate detail. There were ice orchids growing at the feet of silver birch trees sculpted from snow. She gently touched a tiny cup-like flower that looked as if it were blown pink glass, and it tinkled. She spied frost fungus and snow mushrooms emerging from nooks in gnarled and knotted tree roots. Further along the path was an enclosed dell, carpeted with nodding snowdrops. In it a bone-white hummingbird was dipping its slender beak into the bell of a yellow flower blooming on a creeper with pearly leaves.

'I knew you'd come here,' said a cold voice. 'That's why we didn't chase you.'

Bianca stumbled backwards in shock.

Standing below an icy lemon tree, bearing glassy fruit, was Jack. His strange, opal eyes seemed to bore into her. She took in the porcelain detail of the fine chin, thin nose and wild white hair, and knew this figure in front of her was as real as the flowers in this garden.

'What have you done with Casper?'

'Do not worry about him. He is with his winter creature.'

'You trapped Pordis in a cage.'

'Yes.' Jack nodded. 'It is you that I must deal with.'

'Who are you?' Bianca asked.

'Who am I?' Jack gave a mirthless chuckle. 'I have many names. Sometimes I am a giant.' The stick-thin body in front of her expanded, growing impossibly tall. 'I have been a mother –' a curving womanly figure now appeared as the giant shrank – 'called Mrs Holle.' A long beard of ice sprouted from the lady's face. 'I have been a grandfather, and many other things besides.' The form and features of the creature in front of her returned to the ones Bianca recognized. 'But you would call me Jack Frost.'

Awe and fear obliterated every thought in Bianca's head.

'How d'you like my garden?' Jack asked, seeming genuinely interested in her answer.

'It's beautiful,' Bianca replied truthfully, feeling every muscle in her body straining to run away. She knew now that she had been foolish. She couldn't foil the plans of Jack Frost! And yet . . . Pitter and Patter had been worried she might. She stalled for time. 'How do you get the colour in the ice?'

'Ice is a crystal. It refracts light,' Jack replied, and, seeing that this wasn't enough explanation, went on. 'Light is all colours. Make the crystal a certain shape

and it will favour a part of the spectrum, giving a petal a blush of colour.'

'I want my brother back,' Bianca blurted out.

'I wish you hadn't taken that book,' Jack said with a little shake of the head. 'We can't have brothers and sisters in Winterton.'

'Please.' Bianca could feel herself panicking. She hadn't reckoned with facing something as ancient and powerful as Jack Frost. 'Finn is my little brother. He needs me. I love him. Let him go.'

'*Love*, meaning an intense affection or great liking of?' Jack asked, giving a dictionary definition of the word.

'Love is not just words,' Bianca replied hotly. 'It's much more powerful than that. It's a force that lives in your heart.'

'Love is powerful?' Jack looked interested in this idea.

'Love is the most powerful thing in the world,' Bianca replied defiantly.

'In the human world?'

'In any world.'

'Interesting.' Jack took a moment to consider this, then walked past Bianca, saying, 'Follow me.'

As he moved away from the lemon tree, Bianca noticed that there was a door beyond it, in the wall of the fortress. What struck her was its utterly ordinary modern shape and appearance. It looked out of place in the exquisite garden of frost flowers.

'You may see Finn and say your goodbyes,' Jack said, walking away. 'Then you will go back.'

'Go back?' Bianca spun round.

'You cannot stay in Winterton. Your memory might spoil all my hard work. And, besides, it would be cruel to take two hearts from a family. You must think of your parents.'

19

SACRIFICE TO ISHILD

'**I** don't understand!' Bianca grabbed at Jack's coat. 'Why are you freezing children's hearts?'

She cried out as the hand that clutched the cloth of Jack's coat tails became translucent as ice. Letting go, she stared in shock at her fingers as they became pink and fleshy once again.

'*I* am not freezing your hearts,' Jack replied calmly. 'You read *The Vanishing World*. You opened your heart to winter. You called for the Snow Queen to come. You invited her in.'

'I . . .' A memory of the spellbinding words inside the silver book appeared in Bianca's mind, and she knew she had uttered them: *I wish the Snow Queen would come. The world is too hot . . . Please come, Snow Queen. My heart longs for you. It's yours. Take it. Make it snow. Make it snow. Make it snow.*

'That book was a trap,' Bianca protested. 'None of us knew what was going to happen to us.'

'Shall we go and find Finn?' Jack turned away.

'Answer me!' Bianca shouted. 'What do you want with our hearts?'

'Are you blind, Bianca?' Jack's voice became a melancholy whisper. 'Do you not see what is happening around you?' Leaning down, Jack forced her to look into his unreadable eyes. 'Winter is dying, Bianca. Our time gets shorter every year. You humans have made the world a place in which we cannot survive.'

'No, I . . .' Bianca gasped in breathless protest.

'The first to go will be the queen, bringer of snow, but I will soon follow. Then it will be farewell to Pitter's hail and Patter's sleet. Quilo will become summer's minion, no longer blowing cold, but hot.' A tilt of the head. 'I know you understand. We're the same, you and I. You're here to save your brother, Finn. I am saving my sister, Ishild.'

Jack's words blasted into Bianca's core, and her mind reeled at the revelation that she'd been spying on and fleeing from Frost, Hail, Sleet and the North Wind.

'That is the story *The Vanishing World* tells,' Jack explained. 'You and every other child in Winterton read it and recognized the truth. That is why you offered up your heart to the Snow Queen. You gave your heart to make it snow.' A sigh suggested this was a rare and wonderful thing. 'Finn was the first to give his heart, so that Ishild might live. He is special. From his imagination I plucked Winterton. That is why he can never leave.'

'Please don't take Finn's heart,' Bianca begged. 'Please.'

'We take nothing,' Jack replied. 'He gives it freely.' He drew himself up. 'If anything, I have been benevolent. Especially considering what humanity has done to me. In exchange for their hearts, the ice children will live here, in wonderful Winterton, playing happily forever, and they will never be sad because they will never remember their past lives. It's every child's dream.'

'Wait!' Bianca reached out to grab Jack, but stopped herself just in time. 'There isn't only a story in that silver book. I saw you put something in there. "Mirror splinters", Pitter said.' She leaned forward as close as she dared. 'What was it? Why did you do that?'

'That? Oh . . . that was nothing.' It was the first time Bianca had seen Jack ruffled.

'Then you can tell me what it was.'

'It was merely a mirror splinter.' Jack pivoted and stalked away from her, out of the frost garden.

Bianca's mind whirled as she hurried after him. *A mirror splinter? Why is there a mirror splinter in each book?*

'Shall we take Finn's favourite route to the throne room?' Jack said in a perkier tone once they'd got to the passageway. 'I made this for him when he first arrived at Snow Haven.' Pointing a finger at the opening of a slide that Bianca could have sworn hadn't been there when she'd passed this way earlier, Jack said, 'Climb inside. Let's ride the Snow Haven Slide.' Grabbing the top of the slide, Jack jumped in, disappearing with a *whoosh*.

Bianca stared down the slide, paralysed by indecision. She didn't want to climb inside. Where might she end up? In the dungeons, perhaps. She only had Jack's word that Casper was with Monodon. And then Monodon's warning came back to her: *'There's something terrible in Snow Haven. Something dying.'* And she was stunned, understanding all of a sudden that it was winter itself, the season of death, that was dying. Her adversaries – Frost, Snow, Hail, Sleet and the North Wind – were winter's elements. They were more ancient and powerful than gods, yet they were fighting for their very existence.

The Earth needs winter, she thought. *I don't want it to disappear. I love winter.*

Bianca climbed into the mouth of the slide. 'Once I've rescued Finn, I will find a way to save winter,' she whispered fiercely. 'If they must take a heart, then let it be mine.'

Drawing in a deep breath to steady her nerves, she gripped the side of the slide and pushed herself off.

The ice curving around her glowed blue. At first, the descent was gentle, but she soon picked up speed as the slide dropped steeply, before being whisked upwards, carried by the momentum of her fall, speeding so fast she was barely touching the surface at all. A sharp turn sent her slithering up the wall, then corkscrewing down, round and round until she was deliriously dizzy. She gasped as the roof of the slide disappeared, showcasing a cloudless blue sky. Fighting gravity, she raised her head a little, and saw she was whirling around the outside of one of the giant towers. Plunging down suddenly, wailing at the thrill of rocketing out of control round another bend, Bianca finally gave in to the joy of sliding, letting herself go as she plunged into darkness, speeding round bends and down until she shot out into a huge mound of soft, fluffy snow.

20

THE RIDDLE

The slide had delivered Bianca into a cavernous hall. The ice walls were intricately carved into a forest mural depicting skeletal trees devoid of leaves.

'You won't be able to take Finn with you when you go,' Jack said matter-of-factly as a breathless Bianca struggled dizzily to her feet. 'He is the Snow Queen's favoured one. But you will get to say goodbye.'

'I'm not going anywhere without Finn,' Bianca replied obstinately. 'He was my brother first and he's *my* favourite one.'

'We'll see.' A whisper of a smile played across Jack's lips. 'I suspect you won't be able to stop yourself.'

Jack's confidence made Bianca nervous. She felt as

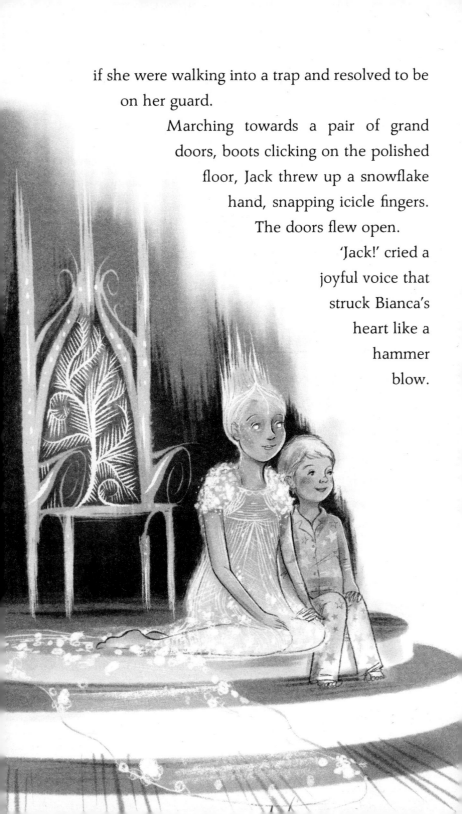

if she were walking into a trap and resolved to be on her guard.

Marching towards a pair of grand doors, boots clicking on the polished floor, Jack threw up a snowflake hand, snapping icicle fingers. The doors flew open.

'Jack!' cried a joyful voice that struck Bianca's heart like a hammer blow.

Running past Jack, she burst into a room with a dais at one end. On it sat an elegant throne that appeared to be carved from bone and studded with diamonds. In front of the throne, sitting on the floor, was an extraordinarily beautiful girl. Her hair stood up in pointy blue icicles and was crowned with a twinkling tiara. Her dress looked to be made of the finest lace. She was holding hands with a blond boy in navy starred pyjamas, and they were laughing as a snow hare leaped around performing somersaults in front of them.

'Finn!' Bianca cried out. She was about to run to her brother when Jack held out an arm to stop her.

'Her Majesty, Queen Ishild, bringer of snow.' Bowing low to the girl on the floor, Jack shot a blank look at Bianca, indicating with a tiny nod that she was to do the same.

Bianca dropped into an awkward curtsy.

'Rise,' a soft voice said inside Bianca's head.

But Bianca stumbled forward, falling to her knees before her brother. 'Oh, Finn, I've found you at last! Are you all right?'

'Hello.' Finn had a distant look in his blue eyes. 'I'm all right, thank you. How are you?'

'Finn, it's me.' Bianca searched his face for signs of recognition.

'Who are you?'

'Bianca, your big sister.' Her heart sank. 'Don't you remember?'

'She's funny.' Finn flashed his toothless smile at the beautiful girl holding his hand, and Bianca felt a stab of jealousy. 'Ishild is my big sister.'

Ishild smiled and nodded.

'No!' Bianca said, hurt by the affection she saw in his eyes. 'I'm your sister!'

'I have two sisters,' Finn said, 'but none of them are you. Ishild makes it snow with her thoughts and Patter dances sleet from her feet.' He studied Bianca. 'What can you do?'

'Er . . . nothing,' Bianca admitted, feeling a bubble of grief ballooning inside her chest. 'Finn.' She leaned towards him and noticed Jack step forward protectively. That nervousness gave her hope. Perhaps there was something that she could do that would reach Finn. 'I am Bianca. But you call me Yanka, because when

you were little, you couldn't say the *B*. I . . . We . . .'
A memory of the two of them bouncing on a big bed
came into her mind. 'At home, we play Bonky Smash
together . . .'

Her throat tightened at the thought of home. A
powerfully strong memory of the place suddenly
blossomed in her mind. She almost gasped at the
recollection. She pushed the memory away, searching
her brother's eyes for any sign that he remembered.
She wrung her hands and felt the little red scarf round
her wrist. Pulling it free, she suddenly knew what it
was. 'Look, Finn, this is Sposh's scarf. Your toy rabbit.
You remember Sposh, don't you?' She held it out. 'You
take him everywhere.'

A flash of recognition shifted the faraway look
in Finn's eyes as he took the red scarf. He stared at
Bianca.

'Sposh isn't a rabbit,' Jack said as Ishild pulled Finn
back towards her, tightening her grip on his hand.
'He's a snow hare, and he's not a toy.'

The snow hare who'd been performing tricks when
Bianca had entered the room hopped between her
and Finn.

'Yes,' agreed Finn, his eyes misting over as he tied
the scarf round the hare's neck. 'Here you are, Sposh.
The girl has brought you a lovely red scarf to wear.'

The hare bounced about, delighted. Bianca realized with a sinking feeling that this was Finn's winter creature. What need had he for a toy?

'What have you done to him?' Bianca turned on Jack, getting to her feet, her fists clenched. She shouted, 'Why doesn't he know who I am?'

The hare's ears drooped as the little creature began to shiver.

'Hey!' Finn said, gathering the white snow hare in a cuddle with his free hand. 'Don't you shout at my brother. You're frightening Sposh.' He stroked the hare's long white ears. 'I think you're mean. I don't want you to be my sister! Go away!'

'Jack isn't your brother!' Bianca exclaimed, feeling the bubble of emotion in her chest growing. 'Ishild is not your big sister, Finn. I am!'

'You're a liar.' Finn shook his head, clutching Ishild's hand tightly, and Jack smiled.

Before she knew what she was doing, Bianca had lurched between them and yanked Finn's hand free from Ishild's. 'She is not your sister!'

Ishild made a strange gurgling sound and slumped backwards. Bianca saw with horror that her perfectly symmetrical features were sliding down her face. Her hair and the lacy hem of her dress were dripping. The girl was melting.

'GO AWAY!' Finn shouted at Bianca, grabbing Ishild's hand and hugging it. 'I HATE YOU!'

As Finn held the young Snow Queen's hand, the dripping came to a stop. Ishild lifted her head, and her eyes settled back into their original position. She sat up, smiling tenderly at Finn.

Bianca was awash with panic. Everything she was doing was making the situation worse. This was not how she'd imagined finding Finn. She turned and looked directly into Jack's blank eyes.

'Please don't do this,' she begged. 'I love my brother. I'll do anything. Please.' She had come so far searching for him. Her only thought had been to rescue him and bring him home. She'd assumed that's what he would want too. She'd imagined him being happy to see her, throwing his arms around her so she could whirl him about like they did when they played at home. Home! The memory came again, even stronger than before. She remembered her bedroom and her books. The bubble of sadness and grief grew in her chest until it seemed to push everything else aside. She missed home.

Another memory hit her like a snowplough. An image of her mum and dad asleep on a park bench, leaning against one another, in front of a frozen Finn. She had forgotten them! She had forgotten her parents! The picture was so powerful that she felt her heart

189

shudder. She bent double as it stole her breath. How could she have forgotten them? Her mum had knitted the purple jumper she was wearing. She felt the weight of her left hand and knew her father was holding it.

'Oh!' She gasped as tears flooded into her eyes.

I know my heart can't be turning to ice, she thought, *because it's hurting.*

'I knew you wouldn't be able to stop yourself,' came Jack's gleeful voice.

Tears cascaded from Bianca's eyes and down her cheeks as her body grew heavier and heavier. She collapsed to the floor, looking up at Finn through a blur of tears.

Clutching Finn's hand, the Snow Queen gave Bianca a look of curious pity and leaned towards her. Inside her head Bianca heard the whispered words:

> *'I am old and new.*
> *I am truth and lies.*
> *I'm made from everything and nothing.*
> *I have the power to change the world.*
> *What am I?'*

Darkness descended and in her mind she heard Pordis cry out, *'Bianca!'*

21

THE THAW

Bianca went rigid with shock. She felt as if she'd been plunged deep into the Arctic Ocean. The cold worked through her body, entering her pores, penetrating her muscles and bones. Her ears crackled as if her mouth were full of popping candy. *What is happening to me?* She panicked, attempting to struggle, but her body was too heavy to move. She couldn't lift her eyelids. She wanted to cry out, but her mouth wouldn't open.

She heard muffled voices. Becoming still, she listened.

'HELP! Something's happening over here! Help me!' She recognized her dad's voice. 'Bianca? Bianca, can you hear me?'

Was she back in the city? How could that be?

She had been cast out of Snow Haven! But how?

She remembered Jack's victorious last words: *'I knew you wouldn't be able to stop yourself!'* Stop herself from doing what? She'd been trying to get Finn to remember her when she'd remembered her home and her parents. Was that what had brought her back? Her memories? Was that why Jack didn't want siblings in Winterton? Or was it something else?

Then she recalled Ishild's strange words to her:

> *'I am old and new.*
> *I am truth and lies.*
> *I'm made from everything and nothing.*
> *I have the power to change the world.*
> *What am I?'*

Had it been a spell? Was that what had hurled her out of Snow Haven?

It hadn't sounded like a spell to Bianca.

It sounded like a riddle.

Bianca's heart ached at being torn away from Finn and Pordis. The air she breathed into her lungs now felt warm and damp compared to the crisp, dry atmosphere of Winterton. She longed to be back there

192

with every fibre of her being. Hot tears washed the ice from her eyes.

She heard excited voices, felt hands working to free her legs and torso.

'Bianca, it's Daddy. I'm here. Mummy's here too. We've got you. Just listen to my voice.'

She felt a towel rubbing her legs. A warm cloth wiped her face. She blinked open her eyes and saw her mum looking anguished. There were white streaks in her auburn fringe.

When did Mum's hair go white?

Bianca let her eyes close as the crushing weight of failure overwhelmed her. She'd set out to save Finn, and she was returning empty-handed. Finn hadn't wanted to come home. He didn't remember it. He hadn't known her. How could she tell her parents that? They would never believe that Finn had given his heart to the Snow Queen, that Ishild needed it because the climate was changing, and she was melting.

They hadn't listened to Bianca about the silver book; she knew they would never believe this.

Her body was wrapped in a crinkly foil blanket as she was laid on the ground, her head in her mother's lap. She was shivering so hard that she was shaking uncontrollably.

'Doctor coming through. Please stand aside,' said a

familiar, melancholy voice. Bianca blinked open her eyes. A crowd was looking down at her. There was hope on many of the faces she could see. She couldn't bear to look at them. She closed her eyes again.

The doctor checked her over. 'She'll be all right,' he reported to her parents. 'She's suffering from hypothermia. We need to get her indoors and keep her wrapped in blankets. A warm drink will help, but not too hot.'

Bianca tried to enjoy the sensation of her mum picking the ice out of her hair, but it felt terrible to be here and know all the other children, including Finn, Casper and Sophie, were in Winterton, having pledged their hearts to the Snow Queen.

Quilo's words blew through her mind: '*When the winter solstice arrives, all their hearts will be turned to ice.*'

Bianca opened her eyes, and her mum, seeing that she was trying to speak, leaned down.

'Wh-wh-wh-when . . . is the w-w-winter solstice?'

'Tomorrow, I think,' her mum replied, looking surprised by the question. 'Today is the twentieth of December.'

Bianca gasped. She tried to sit up but found she couldn't. 'The t-t-t-twentieth? H-h-how long have I been gone?'

'You were frozen for sixteen days,' her dad said.

'There are one hundred and ninety frozen children in the park,' her mum added, then corrected herself. 'One hundred and eighty-nine, now that you're free.'

Bianca couldn't believe what she was hearing. She had not spent one full day in Winterton. Time was different there.

She felt a fresh surge of panic. She didn't have long if she wanted to get Finn back and return the frozen children to their families. She needed to find a way to keep winter alive that didn't require the gift of hundreds of icy hearts to Ishild. But how did you save an entire season?

An ambulance arrived. Bianca in her foil blanket was lifted onto a stretcher and wheeled into the back. Her parents got in and the doors were closed.

'Where are we going?' Bianca asked, conscious now that time moved faster in Winterton.

'The hospital,' her mum replied.

'But I'm feeling much better.' Bianca managed to sit up. 'I don't want to go to the hospital. I want to go home. Please?'

Her parents turned to look at the medic.

'I can check her vital statistics in the ambulance,' she replied. 'If there are no obvious health risks, I don't see why you can't take care of her at home. You can always bring her to the hospital if you have concerns.'

'Then we'd like to take her home,' her dad said, and Bianca smiled gratefully at him.

When they arrived home, Bianca's parents settled her on the sofa in the living room. Her mum built and lit a fire in the stove to warm the room. Her dad brought her a hot chocolate. Compared to the wonderfully thick and bubbly hot chocolate in Winterton, it tasted like sweet water. Nevertheless, Bianca gulped it down. She could see from their faces that there were questions her parents were holding back from asking. She knew those questions would be about Finn. She felt ashamed that she didn't have the answers they were hoping for.

'We got your note,' her dad said, taking her mum's hand. 'That morning, when we woke up and found you gone, we went looking for you. You weren't at school. I was frightened that you'd be in the park . . . like your brother. When we went to the police station, they said you'd been there. When we finally came home, you were already asleep, but I did as you asked. I sat by your bed. I held your hand. As the clock struck midnight, you rose and left the house. You walked to the park. I walked every step with you. Your eyes were closed the whole time. You were sleepwalking. You went to the rose garden. You went up onto the balls of your feet, you tried to lift your arms above your head, as if you wanted to hug the moon, but I was holding your hand, so you could only lift the other one, and then . . .' He shook his head at the memory. 'It was as if the ice came out of your skin. You were frozen. There was nothing I could do.'

'You held my hand all this time?' Bianca marvelled.

'We took it in turns,' her mum said. 'Your dad held your hand all night, but his fingers went numb and so I took over. One of us has being holding your hand all the time since you were frozen.'

Bianca felt a ball of emotion stick in her throat and hot tears fill her eyes. She gave them a watery smile. 'Thank you.'

'Do you know how it happened? What caused it?' her mum asked gently, and Bianca realized that they still didn't believe what she'd told them about the silver book.

'Your breaking free of the ice will give other parents hope, Bianca,' her dad said.

'How did you do it?' Her mum's face was a picture of expectation.

Bianca couldn't reply. She hadn't been trying to break free. Right now, she wished she was back in Winterton. Here, she was powerless to stop what was happening. And she knew that unless she could figure out a way to stop Ishild from melting forever, before the winter solstice, none of the frozen children would be returning to their families for Christmas. And that included Finn.

22

FAIRY TALES

Unable to answer their questions, Bianca remained silent.

'She's tired,' her mum said, getting up and putting her hand on Dad's arm. 'The doctor said we should let her rest.'

Her dad nodded, rising to his feet and forcing a smile. 'How about I make us all some lunch?'

Mum and Dad left the living room, going into the kitchen and shutting the door. Bianca could hear them talking in low, urgent, undecipherable tones.

She looked around the room, at the fire in the hearth, the family photographs on the mantelpiece, the books on the shelves. She shouldn't be here. She needed to get back to Winterton. But if the winter solstice was tomorrow night, the last silver books would have already been made and given out. It would be impossible to get hold of one now. And she didn't even know if the book would work for her a second time.

Peeling back her blankets, Bianca sat up, putting her feet on the floor and testing her legs. They felt wobbly. She stretched herself as she stood up, careful with her stiff body. Her joints popped and cracked.

Going to the window, she peered through the blinds and saw a crowd of people camped out on the pavement. For a second, she wondered what they were doing out there, then realized they were waiting for news from her. News about their own children. She let the blind snap shut.

Her head ached at the flurry of thoughts whirling around her skull. She wanted to save Finn, and all the frozen children, but to do that she had to find a way to save Ishild. Saving winter felt unimaginably impossible when you were just one eleven-year-old girl, with less than a day to do it.

Bianca sank down onto the rug in front of the fire and stared into the flames. The heat on her cheeks brought to mind the haunting memory of

Ishild's features sliding down her face as she melted. Somehow, the Snow Queen's connection to Finn was sustaining her. Only when Bianca had separated them had Ishild begun to melt.

Bianca thought about what Jack had said, that once Ishild was gone they would follow. She couldn't bear the thought of winter disappearing. It was her favourite season. What would it mean for the snow creatures? If there was no winter in the world, where would they live? How would they eat? She knew they wouldn't survive. If winter departed, then so would Pordis the reindeer and Sposh the snow hare and Monodon the narwhal and Lumi the snow leopard and Grendel the polar bear. Bianca found she was crying. It felt so impossibly hopeless.

The story of *The Vanishing World* came back to her, and she remembered, after reading it, how eagerly she had offered her heart to the Snow Queen. She knew she would do it again, and so, she was sure, would all the Ice Children.

It hadn't been the silver book that had been powerful. The book was just frozen water, after all. It was the story inside the book that had changed her.

She heard Ishild's final words to her.

'I am old and new.
I am truth and lies.
I'm made from everything and nothing.
I have the power to change the world.
What am I?'

The answer to Ishild's riddle was suddenly so clear that Bianca laughed.

'It's a story!' she whispered to herself. 'A story has the power to change the world.'

She looked at the bookcase in the alcove beside the fireplace, scanning spines until she found what she was looking for. A volume of fairy tales. Opening it to the contents page, she ran her finger down the list, flipped to the right page, and began to read.

When she closed the book, Bianca looked thoughtfully at the rectangular cover. Who had decided books should be rectangular? Surely a book could be almost any shape? Something one of the grey twins had said answered her question: *'If you read, you know a book is a door . . .'* Bianca thought this was right. When you opened the cover of a book, you stepped into another world. She sat bolt upright as an idea struck her. She suddenly knew how she might get back into Winterton.

Bianca wouldn't have called what she had in her

head 'a plan', but she knew what she had to do next. She pulled on her coat, which was hanging on the back of a chair drying out by the fire, and wondered what had happened to the yellow dressing gown. Was it still in Winterton? Taking her orange diary and pen from her pocket, she wrote:

> *Dear Mum and Dad,*
> *I'm very sorry for running away again. Please don't be cross with me.*
> *I can't explain what I have to do — it won't make sense — but I've got to try and save the others.*
> *I'll be in the park at midnight, tomorrow night, with Finn.*
> *I love you.*
> *Bianca*
> *X*

Sitting down on the sofa, she pulled on her boots and laid the note on the pillow. She knew it would hurt them, but what else could she do?

Wiping the tears from her eyes, she went to the door and opened it a sliver. The kitchen door was still closed. She tiptoed across the hall and into the downstairs toilet. She couldn't go out the front way.

There were too many people there. The window was small, but she knew she could get out of it. She'd climbed through it in the summer when Mum had locked her house keys inside the car and sent Bianca to open the front door from the inside.

Sliding out of the window backwards, she felt her feet land in a deep drift of snow.

Good, she thought. *The snow will muffle my footsteps.*

Taking care to keep low, Bianca hurried to the gate at the bottom of the garden. It was a struggle to open, because of the snow, but she moved it enough to wriggle through.

Once she was in the alleyway and hidden from her parents' eyes, she began to run.

23

AN IMAGINARY DOORWAY

Bianca forged a path through the bitterly cold city as fast as she could. Making her way south, she took a different route from the one she'd ordinarily use, in case people were looking for her. The deep snow creaked under her feet. It was harder than wading through water and slowed her down, but at least it wasn't slippery. When she got to the bridge over the canal, the frozen water looked like stone, grey and unmoving. There were marks and lines from people skating on its surface. In all her lifetime, Bianca had never known the canal to freeze.

Pushing on, she crossed into the industrial district. Vehicles had cleared the snow from the roads here. Salt had been thrown down. The pavement was icy.

She had to take care where she put her feet.

Driving away the thought of her parents finding her note, Bianca focused on Jack, and the way she'd been cast out of Snow Haven. At first, she'd believed it had happened because she remembered her parents, but after reading the book of fairy tales and the story of the Snow Queen, she realized it had been the combination of her love and her tears that had thawed her heart and sent her home. The Ice Children could not remember their loved ones and so would never melt or cry out the mirror shards freezing their hearts.

As Bianca approached the Downy Falls Bookbinding Factory, she studied it for signs of life. The turquoise glow was gone. It looked derelict. She slid towards it, no longer caring if she were seen, only aware that time was ticking away.

As she approached the factory door, she imagined Pordis was trotting by her side, and it helped her feel brave. She knocked, and then tried the handle. It opened, creaking inwards.

Bianca stepped inside, her heart in her throat. But the factory looked as if Jack, Quilo, Pitter and Patter had never been there. The luminous machine that had produced the glittering books was a rusting pile of junk.

'It doesn't matter,' Bianca muttered to herself. 'I'm not here for their book. I'm here to write my own.'

Hurrying to the staircase, she made her way along the walkway to the middle door. She turned the handle, pushing and pulling at it. It didn't open. Leaning her forehead against it, she summoned the memory of Jack's frost garden and the ordinary door beyond the lemon tree. She felt certain it was a bridge between the two worlds. How else had Jack and the others got here? Well, she knew now that there was more than one way to open a door; they had taught her that.

Bianca sat cross-legged on the floor and took out her orange diary. Turning to a clean page in the notes section, she removed the lid of her pen and cast her mind back to her arrival at Snow Haven, after Pordis had been captured and Casper had bravely chosen a passageway. She pictured the moment Casper had disappeared into the floor, trying to imagine it from his perspective, and lowered her pen to the page. She wrote how it must have felt, the terror and the exhilaration of sliding down into the glacier. Twisting and spinning out of control, Casper hadn't known where he was going. A bright light sped towards him and he shot out of the chute, high above the sea, and then he was falling . . .

'Monodon!' Casper cried out, as he splash-landed and sank beneath the waves.

'*Beneath you, my friend,*' the narwhal replied, rising from the deep. '*I sensed you were coming.*'

Casper grabbed on to Monodon's horn as they rose together, breaking the surface of the sea with a gasp and a snort. Monodon carried Casper to the ice raft. Clambering up, Casper rolled onto his back, gasping for breath.

'*You fell?*'

'I fell into a trap,' Casper said. 'Snow Haven captured

Pordis and then spat me out!'

'*The castle is all snow. It is alive,*' Monodon replied. '*The queen controls it. She is it.*'

'I need to get back up there and help Bianca,' Casper said, rolling onto his knees and coughing out the salt water from the back of his throat. 'If she falls out of the chute, please will you catch her?'

'*For you, I will.*'

Casper stood up and shook himself like a dog, sending water droplets in all directions. 'Right, here I go again,' he said, psyching himself up for the arduous climb back along the ledge, through the rocks and up the slope.

But this time there was no wind to fight and the scramble up the slope was not so tough. He was wondering how he was going to get past the snow golems when he spied figures by the entrance arch to the palace. He dropped down behind a snow-covered boulder and watched.

The snow golems were standing on either side of a sparkling white sleigh the size of a car. It appeared to be carved from ice. Fractal patterns decorated its high curving sides. Inside was a deep seat covered in fluffy snow.

He gasped as a tall, thin figure in a white suit and top hat strode out of the palace holding the reins of a creature that Casper would have thought was a pure white shire horse with a silver mane and tail if there hadn't been a shimmering iridescent horn protruding from its forehead.

'A unicorn!' he whispered in awe.

The snow golems hooked the unicorn up to the sleigh, and Casper took advantage of their being busy to creep closer, dodging from boulder to boulder.

The thin white figure returned with a boy in a bear suit and a pair of twins dressed in grey.

The boy in the bear suit climbed into the driving seat of the sleigh and took the unicorn's reins. The other three children lined up as a beautiful wraithlike girl glided out of the palace in a dress of snowflake lace, wearing a crown of diamonds. She was clutching the hand of a little blond boy dressed in navy starred pyjamas. He was accompanied by a bouncing snow hare.

Casper swallowed. He was almost certain he was looking at Bianca's little brother. But where was *she*?

Taking the white-suited child's hand, the girl climbed into the sleigh. Bianca's brother got in and sat next to them with his snow hare. The grey twins clambered into the seat in front, sitting either side of the boy in the bear suit.

The golems collapsed into heaps of snow that rippled like a wave to raise the sleigh, as the boy in the bear suit blew a great gust of wind under the hooves of the unicorn, lifting it into the air as it trotted forward.

Casper watched in wonder as the sleigh flew up and away from Snow Haven.

Remembering his mission, he sprinted towards the giant archway, expecting that at any second a golem would rise up in front of him and bar his way – but he made it.

'Pordis?' he called out, looking up at the cage suspended in the porch roof. 'You still up there?'

Hearing the clatter of hooves above him, Casper went back outside and looked around. He found a big rock that he could just about move, and rolled it into the porch until it leaned against the wall to which the chain was attached. Climbing onto it, he was able to reach the wheel that held the chain. He yanked at it and pushed it, but it didn't move. Jumping down, he ran back outside, searching for something that would help, and spotted a sharp-edged flint. He grabbed it and ran back to the rock. Clambering up, using both hands, he brought the sharp edge of the flint down on the chain with all his strength, again and again, until the ice link shattered, and the cage dropped. It made a terrible racket as the chain spooled down. The ice cage hit the floor with a *bang!*, shattering and falling apart.

Pordis snorted as she jumped free, giving him an accusatory look.

'Sorry.' Casper shrugged apologetically. 'It was the only thing I could think of.'

Pordis shook her antlers, and Casper wasn't sure whether she was cross or forgiving him.

'Bianca's in here somewhere. We must find her.'

But Pordis was already trotting towards the passageway that Casper had first chosen.

'No, not that way. It's a trap.'

Pordis ignored him, prancing over the hole that Casper had fallen into and continuing up the hall. Casper had no choice but to follow the reindeer.

When they arrived in the frost garden, Casper gazed around in amazement, but Pordis took the edge of his pyjama top between her teeth and pulled him through the garden until he stood beside a lemon tree in front of an ordinary-looking door.

The reindeer pawed her hoof against the door.

'Is Bianca behind this door?' Casper asked.

Pordis nodded.

'Then we'd better work out how to open it.' Casper ran his hands over its surface. There was no handle or lock. It felt like a sheer rectangular wall of ice.

Casper took a step back, studying the door. He fancied he could see a dark shape through it. The harder he looked, the clearer the shape became, until he could see it was Bianca, in her purple jumper and coat, sitting cross-legged on the other side of the door, writing in a small orange book. He focused his attention on her, and the image grew sharper until the door was as transparent as water. Following a sudden instinct, Casper reached both his hands through the glassy surface and made a grab for her.

24

THE SNOW CIRCUS

Bianca pushed her imagination to describe every vivid detail of her story, and, as she saw a pair of brown hands reach through the door, she dropped her orange book, grabbed them and hurled herself forward, back into Snow Haven.

'Watch it!' Casper cried out as Bianca collided with him, knocking him off his feet. The pair of them landed on a carpet of snowdrops.

'It worked!' Bianca exclaimed, sitting up and looking about in astonishment. 'I'm back!'

'Hold still,' Casper said, gently lifting an icy ladybird with blue spots from her cheek. He held it up so she could see it. The ladybird flicked open its spotted elytra and launched itself into the air.

Bianca gave him a spontaneous hug. 'Thank you for coming to get me.'

''S all right,' Casper muttered, suddenly bashful. 'What're friends for?'

'Oh, Pordis!' Bianca flung her arms round the reindeer. 'I've missed you.'

'*And I you.*' The reindeer nuzzled Bianca's neck.

'How long have I been gone?'

'*Moments have passed.*'

'But how many minutes?'

'*What is minutes?*'

'About twenty,' replied Casper. 'Maybe half an hour.'

'We don't have much time. We need to find Jack.'

'Is Jack the tall, thin one? Wears a top hat?'

'Yes.'

'Jack's gone. They all have. They got into a big sleigh pulled by a unicorn. And, Bianca . . .' Casper swallowed. 'They've got Finn.'

'Yes, I know.' Bianca nodded.

Casper was surprised by her calm reaction to this news.

'Did you see which way they went?' Bianca asked.

'It looked like they were heading to Winterton.'

'Then that's where we need to go,' Bianca said, hurrying out of the frost garden. 'We need to reach them as quickly as we can.'

'Monodon will take us,' Casper said, picking up his pace as Bianca started running.

'When you fell, did the slide take you down to Monodon?' Bianca asked as they sprinted down the passageway.

'Yes, but—'

'Great.' As she approached the hole, Bianca dived down it head first. 'Meet you by the ice raft, Pordis,' she called out as she zoomed away down the slide.

Bianca whooped as she shot out of the slide, bringing her arms and legs together into a dive. She heard Casper's whoop of delight as he rocketed out of the chute above her. He hit the water seconds after she did.

Monodon was waiting. The whale swam to Bianca so she could grab on to his horn, before collecting Casper. When they arrived at the ice raft, Pordis was climbing aboard. Bianca pulled herself out of the water, marvelling that she didn't feel the cold here. Monodon moved around to the shore side and pushed their Arctic craft back towards the Winterton cove.

'Casper, look.' Bianca pointed. Snow Haven was bathed in a delicate lilac-pink wash of colour. 'The sun is setting.'

'It's not done that before.' Casper looked at

her. 'Does it mean something?'

'It means time is running out. The winter solstice is starting.'

Casper closed his eyes to speak to the narwhal, and Monodon's tail beat the water faster, propelling them forward at a ferocious speed.

As their sheet of ice approached the beach, Bianca, Casper and Pordis jumped ashore. Bianca climbed aboard her reindeer's back, then held out her hand to Casper. 'Pordis says she will carry you.'

The stoic reindeer cantered up the rocky path with the two children on her back.

'Where are we going?' Casper asked as they passed under the sign for Winterton.

'To find Jack,' Bianca replied. 'The sleigh you described should be easy to spot.'

There were a few children on the rides, but most of them were moving away from the fairground towards the snowball field, and Bianca could hear music being played on whistles. She and Casper slid off Pordis's back and they joined the crowd, moving past a brightly painted open-sided wagon.

Inside the wagon, Quilo was playing the keyboard of a calliope, a steam organ. He looked delighted with himself as he played his merry tune, calling all the children to their next and final entertainment.

The snowball field had been transformed from a battleground into an amphitheatre. Rising tiers of snow seats fanned out around the stage, an enormous circular disc of ice. A chain of cheerful pink lanterns was suspended between tall posts encircling the arena. Children and their winter creatures were flooding into the theatre with mugs of hot chocolate and punnets of frozen fruit. The seats were filling up fast. Behind the circular stage was a blazing backdrop saying SNOW CIRCUS, and Bianca saw a trapeze above the stage.

This is where they're going to collect the frozen hearts for Ishild, she thought, searching the crowd for Jack's tall, thin figure.

'The sleigh is behind the stage.' Casper pointed. 'I can see the back of it.'

'That must be where Jack is,' Bianca said.

Casper moved to go with her, but Bianca stopped him. 'Casper, I . . . I need to talk to Jack alone.'

'But what if you get trapped again? Jack is dangerous and they've got your brother.'

'If I need help, Pordis will come and get you.' Bianca tried to sound as if she knew what she was doing.

Casper studied her grave face and frowned. 'This isn't just about your brother, is it?'

'No.' Bianca felt a flash of guilt. Casper had no idea that his heart was in jeopardy, that there was another world in which he had a dad who loved him dearly and wanted his son back. 'It's bigger than that. It's bigger than all of us. It's too big to explain.' The music from the calliope wagon was getting louder as two enormous polar bears dragged it onto the stage. Quilo was standing up on his seat as he played, acting like a rock star. 'I don't have time to tell you the whole story. The show is starting.'

'You go,' Casper said, stepping back. 'I'll get a seat as close to the front as I can. In case you need me.'

Bianca shot him a grateful smile and ran down the field, heading for the backdrop behind the circular stage. There were no guards. She guessed that, with her safely gone from Winterton, Jack and the others thought they didn't need them. All the other children were in thrall to winter.

Slipping behind the backdrop, a woven tapestry of snowflakes, Bianca found herself in a backstage area. Four tall, thin white tents were pitched in a semicircle, their doorways decorated with triangular flags of pale smoke, fluttering without a breeze. The sleigh, with the unicorn still tethered to it, was parked in front of them.

Bianca felt drawn to the unicorn. How magical would it feel to touch its silver mane and look deeply into its eyes? But she was on an urgent quest. She turned her attention to the four tents. Peering in the first, she saw it was empty, and guessed it was Quilo's as he was on the stage. A noise startled her and, quick as a flash, she slipped inside, peeping through the gap in the fabric. She saw Jack, wearing a white ringmaster's jacket with tails, a white top hat and carrying a silver cane, stride past. After a moment's hesitation, she came out of hiding, opening her mouth to speak, only to see Jack leap impossibly high, rising above the tapestry backdrop. Reaching out a snowflake hand, his fingertips shot out ice, making a path in the air. Holding the silver cane high, Jack Frost slid down the path as it was created. 'Children! Creatures of winter! Welcome to the Snow Circus!'

The audience cheered, clapped, honked and howled.

Running to the backdrop, Bianca looked under it and saw Jack descend onto the circular stage where Quilo was playing a wild tune on the steam organ.

'Let us begin,' Jack cried, 'with the winter animal parade!'

And all the snow creatures, whom the children loved so dearly, filed down to the stage to march around in time to Quilo's mad music, while the children whooped and applauded them.

The show had begun, and Bianca didn't know how to stop it.

25

A BETTER ENDING

Jack strode back into the tent, a ripple of wild applause and music sweeping in behind.

Bianca was waiting for him.

'How on earth did you get here?' Jack looked shocked. 'It's not possible. Every book is accounted for!'

'I wrote a new story,' Bianca replied, unable to keep a hint of pride from her voice. 'I found your door between the worlds and opened it with words and my imagination. I've changed the plot. I am a part of winter's story. You cannot keep me out.'

'Congratulations.' Jack clapped sardonically. 'But you're too late. There's nothing you can do.' Snowflake hands gestured to the theatre. 'Their hearts are all but frozen. Now go away. We've got a show to put on.'

'I came here to help you,' Bianca said, unmoving.

Jack stiffened, looking at her with suspicion.

Bianca drew herself up. 'There is a flaw in your plan.'

'Oh, the plan will work,' Jack insisted.

'For *this* winter.' Bianca nodded. 'Perhaps the next one. But for how long?' She paused, knowing it must be a question Jack had pondered. 'Can the frozen hearts of two hundred children keep Ishild alive indefinitely, when the planet is getting warmer all the time?'

'It will stop her from dying now.' Jack's voice cracked, and Bianca could hear the fear and grief.

'For now,' Bianca said softly, 'but then what will you do?'

Jack didn't reply, instead going to the mirror framed with light bulbs and removing his white top hat.

'You'll never be able to make enough silver books to sustain Ishild forever,' Bianca said, taking a step closer. 'You must know that?'

'Every time this planet cycles round the sun, Ishild is diminished.' Jack's head drooped and Bianca could see the toll this fight for winter was taking. 'I am the frost that lives in the liminal shift between autumn and winter, winter and spring.' Jack gave a half-hearted theatrical hand wave. 'I am the Snow Queen's herald.

I go before her, announcing her arrival. When she no longer graces the Earth, neither will I.'

'None of us want that, Jack.' Bianca moved nearer, wishing she could reach out, but knowing she couldn't touch the frosty figure. 'The Earth needs winter.'

'Ha!' Jack's head snapped back angrily. 'Your factories belching hot gas into the sky tell a different story. Humans are burning this planet, heating it by degrees, driving us out.' Jack's lips curled into a sneer, showing a glimpse of needle teeth. 'Look at the melting glaciers and the shrinking ice plains.'

'But you must know how wonderful we think winter is,' Bianca countered. 'You saw it when you created Winterton for us.'

'I know how wonderful *children* think winter is,' Jack conceded. 'They see the joy and beauty of it. They don't fear the cold. That is why we made the silver books for them – and them alone. They are willing to make a sacrifice. Many fully grown humans are no longer close to nature. They would not consider it.'

'It's like that fairy story about the selfish giant,' Bianca said, nodding. 'Except humans are the selfish giant that won't let others play in our garden.'

'The Earth, contrary to what you believe, is not *your* garden,' Jack snapped.

'You're right,' Bianca said softly. 'I was thinking of a story.'

'I know the one.' Jack nodded.

'It was Ishild's riddle that helped me understand how you are freezing our hearts,' Bianca explained. 'The mirror splinters you put in the silver books, they're from her story, aren't they? The story of *The Snow Queen*.'

'When I used to visit your houses to paint frost ferns on your windows, after dark, I would listen to the bedtime stories parents read their children,' murmured Jack. 'I've heard many tales over thousands of years. My favourites were the wintry ones.'

'Is that how you heard *The Snow Queen*?'

'Yes. The tale told of a magic mirror, created by a devil to play a trick on the angels. It reflected beautiful and good things as ugly and evil. You could be eating delicious ice cream, but looking in the mirror would make it appear and taste like dog poop.' Jack chuckled. 'When the mirror was finished, the devil sent it to the angels, hoping they would look in it and see themselves as horrible. But the mirror slipped from his servant's grasp and fell to Earth, shattering into a million pieces. Some of the tiniest pieces got lodged in people's eyes, and they saw the world as a grim place.'

'And some people got splinters in their hearts, and

their hearts became lumps of ice,' Bianca finished. 'But the mirror isn't real. It's from a story.'

'What is real? Is Winterton real?' Jack raised an eyebrow. 'I looked into the hearts of the heartless. I found shards of that mirror. I've been collecting them for more than a hundred years. Ever since the Arctic started warming.' Though Jack's eyes were blank, Bianca read sadness there. 'You saw my sister in Snow Haven. She is weak. I have no other way to make her strong. I will not let Ishild die.' A snowflake hand gestured to Winterton. 'This is not cruel. The children have forgotten their past lives. They are happy. Their winter spirit animal is made flesh, so they have a best friend to play with.'

'Winter spirit animal?'

'Yes. Inside the soul of every human are the spirits of four creatures that express your connection to each season. They are a part of you. Winterton makes your winter spirit animal flesh. It's part of the magic of this place.'

Pordis! thought Bianca. *You are my winter!* And she smiled, knowing it was true.

'Jack. What will happen at midnight on the winter solstice?' Bianca asked.

'The children will willingly give their frozen hearts to Ishild. They will die in the real world, but they will live on in Winterton forever.'

'Never growing or getting older?' Bianca tried to hide her horror, as thoughts of her grieving parents filled her head.

'They will be ice figments,' Jack replied. 'Elemental creatures of winter, like me.'

'Jack, I want to help you save winter, I really do,' Bianca insisted. 'But this isn't the way.'

'You do not want to help me. You are here for yourself, to take back your brother from Ishild.'

'You're wrong, Jack,' Bianca said, desperate to explain what she knew to be true. 'I'm scared of the planet getting warmer. If the climate changes and the polar ice caps melt, seas will rise and the world won't be safe for any of us.'

The music from the circus stage ended. Bianca's heartbeat accelerated as she heard delighted howls, cheers and the clatter of footsteps, mixed with applause.

'Then you understand why I must do this.' Jack stepped towards the door of the tent.

'No.' Bianca moved to block the doorway.

A white eyebrow lifted.

'Taking their hearts tonight won't save winter forever.'

'There is no other way,' said Jack.

'But there is,' Bianca insisted. 'You have to listen to me. Children are powerful. We are the future grown-ups. The people we decide to become, the things we choose to do with our lives – that will change the world.' She looked at the immobile features of Jack's thin face, hoping to see her words sinking in. 'To save winter, we need to change the hearts of the whole human race. You can't do that by freezing the hearts of children. It will make adults want to destroy winter. It will start a war.'

Jack's lips formed a stubborn line. 'If it's a war they want, then so be it.'

'No! Jack! Ishild's riddle was right. Stories *can* change the world. They change the future by changing the minds and the hearts of people who read and hear them. They are powerful enchantments. And those who listen and read best, most wholeheartedly, are children . . .'

'You're stalling, to try and save your brother,' Jack snarled, pushing past her, and throwing back the tent flap. Bianca saw a ripple of green and purple light in the dark sky behind him. 'The aurora borealis is dancing. The heart-giving ceremony is almost upon us.'

'You must listen to me, Jack.' Bianca grabbed the figure of Frost, gasping as her hands turned to ice, but not letting go. 'There is only one way to save winter, and that is to make all humans love it, see the importance of it, the sacredness of it. We have winter spirit animals because we are a part of winter and winter is a part of us.' Her impassioned words came from the very centre of her soul and rang with truth. 'If you take our hearts, you will be turning winter into a villain. Something to be beaten, thwarted and extinguished. You'll be turning your wonderful sister into an evil queen who steals children's hearts and eats them. Do you want those to be the bedtime stories you hear at windows?' she cried. 'Don't you see? We must come up with a better ending.'

'Enough!' Jack broke free of her grip, knocking Bianca to the ground, and strode out of the tent. 'It's too late.'

26
THE PROMISE

How many heartbeats does Finn have left in the real world? Bianca thought as she ran out of the tent, her frozen hands slowly thawing. Jack had vanished. Cursing, she hurried to the stage and lifted the woven backdrop.

All the children in the theatre had their mouths open and were looking up. Pitter and Patter were performing a death-defying trapeze routine, flinging each other into the air and catching one another as their swings rocketed forwards and backwards. She saw Pitter hurled upwards by Patter. He pretended to swim through the air, hovering, defying gravity for an impossible moment as the sky above him glowed with the soft, shifting colours of the Northern Lights.

And then he fell into a tumble, roly-polying towards the ground. Patter swung down and grabbed his feet when he was barely a metre from the icy stage.

The children roared their approval, leaping to their feet and applauding.

'Pordis, I need you,' Bianca whispered, crawling under the cloth. Getting to her feet, she immediately felt vulnerable, standing at the back of the huge stage. Everyone could see her.

'*I am coming*,' Pordis replied.

Standing there, Bianca's heartbeat accelerated. She felt impossibly small, searching the crowd for familiar faces. Where had Jack gone? She didn't know what she was going to do, but she knew she had to do something to change the ending of Jack's story. She immediately felt braver when she saw Pordis, her winter spirit animal, leap onto the stage. The reindeer trotted over to her.

'*I am here.*'

Two grey figures dropped from the sky, landing in front of Bianca and Pordis, barring their way.

'Where d'you think you're going?' Patter asked snarkily.

'What seeds are you sowing?' Pitter leered at her.

Bianca gave them her most innocent smile. 'I'm here to see you dance. My brother says that when

231

you do, hail and sleet fall from the skies, and that it's one of the most awesome sights in the world.'

Pitter and Patter both seemed to grow taller.

'Your brother is right.'

'Our dancing is a sight . . .'

'. . . that you must behold . . .'

'. . . before you grow old!'

And the pair tapped a slow, sharp beat with their right feet on the icy floor of the stage.

The audience fell silent with anticipation, and Pitter and Patter couldn't resist turning to face them. They hopped with a skip, jump, tip, tap, forward and back, to the middle of the stage.

The children started to clap in time.

Pitter and Patter chanted a poem as they danced.

'Come –' *tippety-tap* – 'winter –' *tip-tap* – 'come . . .' *Skippety-snap.*

'. . . with –' *tippety-tap* – 'dazzling –' *tip-tap* – 'low sun.' *Skippety-snap.*

A barrage of hailstones fell from the skies in a neat circle around them, landing on the stage and creating a soft rhythmic accompaniment. The audience murmured with wonder at this neat trick.

'Decorate branches and bowers . . .'

'. . . with crystalline flowers.'

Skippety-snap, tap-tap.

'Creep –' *tippety-tap* – 'frost –' *tip-tap* – 'creep . . .'
Skippety-snap.

'. . . while –' *tippety-tap* – 'we –' *tip-tap* – 'all sleep.'
Skippety-snap.

'Your breath becomes mist . . .'

'. . . when the earth is frost-kissed.'

Skippety-snap, tap-tap.

'Fall –' *tippety-tap* – 'snow –' *tip-tap* – 'fall . . .'
Skippety-snap.

'Blanket –' *tippety-tap* – 'us –' *tip-tap* – 'all.' *Skippety-snap.*

'Silence life's thrum . . .'

'. . . its buzz, tweet and hum.'

Skippety-snap, tap. Tippety-tap, tap.

Crat-tickity, ga-ga-skippety – 'HA!' they both cried,
their arms above their heads, hailstones and sleet
flying from their fingertips and raining down on the
stage.

The audience exploded into rapturous applause.

Bianca didn't give herself time to think. She put her
hand on Pordis's neck and marched into the middle of
the stage. It was now or never.

'Are you ready to meet Her Majesty, Ishild, the
Queen of Snow?' Bianca cried, not certain what words
might fly out of her mouth. Her body was trembling,
and she leaned against Pordis for support. She spotted

Casper as he leaped in the air and shouted 'YES!',
beginning a response that rippled around the theatre.
He was in the front row to her right.

Pitter and Patter looked at Bianca with confused

expressions. They hadn't expected her to say that.

Lifting her chin, Bianca pronounced in a loud clear voice, 'There once was a time of great harmony,' and Winterton seemed to vibrate as if a giant string had been plucked. 'And we are the Ice Children, destined to bring about a time like that again! AREN'T WE?'

There was a roar of approval from the audience.

From the corner of her eye, Bianca could see Pitter and Patter quarrelling. Pitter pointed two fingers at his sister and shot a ball of hail at her in frustration. Patter opened her mouth and shot a stream of sleet into his face.

'Behind this very stage, the Snow Queen is waiting to meet you all,' continued Bianca putting her hand to her ear. 'Are you excited?'

There was a loud cheer of 'Yes!'

'I can't hear you!'

'YES!' screamed the children.

'Who here loves snow?' Bianca cried, finding her stride.

'ME!' shouted Casper.

'I do!' Gwen put a hand in the air.

'I like it best!' cried Sophie Lilley.

'Who loves ice cream and slushy drinks?' Bianca asked. 'Hot chocolate and holidays? Festivities and singing carols?' She fired out the questions without leaving any gaps for answers. 'Who loves skiing and snowboarding? Ice skating? Snowball fights, sledging, snow angels and snowmen?' She paused. 'Who loves WINTER?'

She'd worked them up into a frenzy. The children were all on their feet now, jumping about, screaming and shouting. Polar bears were clapping. Penguin flippers were flapping. And the aurora borealis came in waves of emerald and magenta light above their heads.

'But *tonight* —' Bianca raised her hands — 'may be the last time you ever get to see the Snow Queen.'

The clamour immediately dropped to a concerned chatter.

'Because winter is in trouble, my friends. It needs our help.'

Suddenly it was so silent, you could have heard a single hailstone fall.

'Her snow cannot settle. The skies are so warm that glaciers are melting and falling into the sea. Daffodils that shouldn't appear till spring pop up in December. Seasons are merging and breaking apart, confusing wildlife.'

'We must do something!' Casper cried, loud and clear, piercing the concerned clamour.

'We *are* going to do something,' Bianca said, grateful

for Casper's support. 'We are going to SAVE IT!'

Out of the corner of her eye, she saw an angry-looking Jack yank Pitter and Patter off the stage.

'Each of you is here because you are special.' Bianca turned her head, taking in every child. 'You love winter. You have been chosen to be one of the Snow Queen's Ice Children.'

'*Ice Children! Ice Children! Ice Children!*' Casper started chanting, and the crowd joined in.

Bianca glanced nervously at the side of the stage. Jack was standing with arms crossed, staring at her.

'Each of you will tell your friends, your brothers and sisters, your cousins, of the things we must do to save winter. We will create a world of Ice Children who will do all they can to make this planet a place where winter is respected, celebrated even. We may be young, but there are many millions of us on this planet. We are the future, and we can make a difference.' She tipped back her head and shouted with her whole heart. 'WE WILL MAKE A DIFFERENCE!'

'YES!' shouted the Ice Children.

'I will. I promise to protect it,' came the cacophony of calls. 'Me too. I love winter!'

'Inside the heart of every Ice Child lives your winter spirit animal, reminding you of what we're fighting for.' Bianca put her arm around Pordis. 'Together, we

WILL save winter.' She punched her fist into the air.

The mood of the crowd had changed. It was focused and urgent, quick to listen and respond to her cues.

'It is a tradition of nature that winter is heralded by a very special someone.' She opened out her arms. 'Please give a wonderfully cold welcome to the one and only . . . Jack Frost!' Bianca pointed to Jack as she retreated to the opposite side of the stage, leaving the platform for the figure of Frost. Her heart felt as if it were beating inside her skull. Would it work? Would Jack follow her lead and see that there was another way?

'My friends, children and creatures of winter . . .' Jack's eyes searched the passionate faces of the crowd, then turned a piercing gaze on Bianca.

She held her breath.

Suddenly Jack's hand flew forward, shooting streamers of ice over the heads of the audience. 'She gave the Earth the gift of a crystal flake –' Frost's crackling voice rose like a ringmaster's – 'wrapping her arms around the planet so life might be created. She cleansed the atmosphere of methane, wiped out the dinosaurs and turned this spinning sapphire globe into a giant snowball!' Jack's hands moved as if conducting an invisible orchestra. A towering tsunami of snow rose up behind the backdrop and everyone looked up. Jack's voice grew louder. 'She is a birther of gods, a beginner and ender of life. She is Old Hiam, the Winter King, but you like to imagine her in a dress. Please give it up for Ishild, my big sister and your SNOW QUEEN!'

The children were silent, their mouths open, looking up in awe, too stupefied to be scared. The giant wave of snow looked as if it were about to sweep them all into oblivion . . . when it froze, solidifying, as if time had stopped. A sparkling sleigh crested the wave, and a gentle flurry of flakes accompanied the descent of Ishild. The sleigh swooped down the wave, pulled by the unicorn.

The children erupted, jumping onto their seats and waving. Bianca's heart swelled as she spotted Finn sitting between Ishild and Sposh, waving too. The sleigh slid to a halt in the middle of the stage. The unicorn whinnied, its glistening horn scattering rainbows of coloured light, and the audience sighed.

Jack offered a hand to Ishild, bowing as she stepped lightly from the sleigh, clutching Finn's hand. Sposh tumbled out of the sleigh after them.

Jack dropped to one knee. Quilo, Pitter and Patter moved to the back of the stage and did the same. Bianca copied them, and the audience of Ice Children followed.

A jingle of sleigh bells indicated they could rise, and Bianca gasped to see that the Snow Queen had let go of Finn's hand.

Ishild was hovering in the air above the stage, looking as if she'd been carved from snow by an artist. Over her gown of fine snowflake lace, she wore a short jacket made of frost froth, and her hair stood impossibly

high: pointy blue
stalagmites encircled
by a diamond crown.
Her symmetrical features were
of fairy tale proportions and her big eyes
were devoid of pupils, like Jack's. Bianca thought she
looked like a beautiful doll.

'*My children.*' Her voice, as soft as falling snow,
settled in their minds. '*This girl speaks the truth. If you
cannot keep this world temperate enough for me, then I
will have to leave it.*' She turned her head, bestowing
a benevolent smile on all her Ice Children. '*Tonight
is the winter solstice, the longest night, when I am at my*

strongest, and yet, still, I am melting.'

She gestured to the dripping hem of her skirt, and a concerned murmur could be heard from the children in the theatre.

'We will help you,' Gwen called out, looking distraught. 'Please don't melt.'

'It will take more than the few of you here to make a difference,' the Snow Queen said inside their heads, not needing to raise her voice above the alarmed clamour that was growing in the theatre as her icicle hair wilted. *'It will take every child in the world to restore harmony. But it can be done. One snowflake will melt on its own, but billions of them together –'* her graceful arm lifted, gesturing to the frozen tsunami behind her – *'are powerful enough to change the face of a planet.'*

'We will save you!' Casper cried out. 'I will dedicate my life to it.'

'And me!' said the boy standing beside him.

'I promise,' came a blizzard of voices. 'I swear!'

Bianca came forward, held her hand over her heart, and shouted, 'I, Bianca Albedo, promise I will dedicate my life to saving winter, and will for evermore be one of the Ice Children.'

Other hands covered hearts. She saw Sophie Lilley and Gwen repeat the promise. The whole amphitheatre was reverberating with the words. Bianca turned to see Jack's frosty face shining with wonder and hope.

In the silence that followed, Ishild opened her arms, inviting the children to approach. Finn tried to take her hand, but she shook her head. Bianca could see how much it distressed her brother to see the Snow Queen melting.

Finn's mouth turned down, his eyes filled with tears and then suddenly he vanished, leaving behind a handful of snowflakes dancing in the air like tiny white ballgowns whirling to inaudible music.

Bianca gasped. She had hoped, but not dared believe, that this might happen. The love Finn had for Ishild had warmed his frozen heart. The distress he felt at seeing her melt had made him cry. That was how Jack had forced the mirror shard out of Bianca's heart, and now it was out of Finn's.

She saw Jack go to the spot where Finn had vanished. He bent down, picked up something tiny from the stage and pocketed it.

One after another, the children came to meet their beloved Snow Queen. They wept to see how she struggled to keep her form, and they too vanished, leaving behind only puffs of flakes.

27
REUNITED

'**D**o I have to go?' Casper asked, looking over his shoulder towards the cove. Other than Bianca, he was the only child left in the amphitheatre. 'I want to stay with Monodon.'

'I understand.' Bianca leaned her head against Pordis's neck. 'But our winter spirit animals come from inside us, Casper. When you go back, Monodon will be here.' She placed her hand on his heart. 'And there's someone you love waiting for you back home, longing for you to return.'

'There is?' Casper was surprised.

'Your dad.' Bianca nodded. 'He looks a lot like you. He has the same nose, chin and clever brown eyes, but his hair is silver, and he has a voice as low as the musk ox. He is so sad with you gone.'

Casper's expression turned inward as a memory called to him and his eyes filled with tears. A moment later, he vanished.

'And what about you?' Jack asked, stalking across the stage. 'You have no ice in your heart to be melted. You have no way back.'

'Well . . .' Bianca said, 'I haven't had time to tell you the second part of my plan yet.'

'You're making this up as you go along!' Jack exclaimed.

'Isn't that how all stories are created?' Bianca replied smartly, and Quilo snorted with laughter. 'I made a promise – all the Ice Children did. We need to act on that promise immediately, to stop Ishild from melting. We cannot let everyone think what happened here was some kind of dream. Tomorrow can't be the same as today. Tomorrow is too late. We need to do something right now so that no one will ever forget.'

Ishild smiled at Bianca.

'Yes,' Jack agreed.

Pitter and Patter skipped about excitedly.

'I can make a noise no one will ever forget,' Quilo said.

Pitter and Patter cackled like geese.

'What are you suggesting?' Jack asked Bianca.

'I have an idea,' Bianca replied, 'but it might be impossible.'

'Go on,' Quilo prompted, rubbing his hands together. 'Sounds interesting.'

'Bring our two worlds together,' Bianca said to Jack. 'Just for tonight. Make Winterton appear in my world.'

'It is the winter solstice,' Jack conceded. 'The veil between this place and the city park is very thin right now, and with all the Ice Children returning, their memories of this place will be vivid . . . It's possible.'

'Let's show everyone the wonder of winter,' Bianca said, becoming excited. 'We will make sure they never forget their promise.'

'If you can imagine it, and make it part of the story of the Ice Children,' Jack said, with a flash of needle-sharp teeth, 'I think we could make it happen.'

'If it's to be done . . .' Pitter chanted.

'. . . all the Ice Children must come . . .' Patter continued.

'. . . together as one!' they said in unison.

'Ooh, a reality smoosh,' Quilo exclaimed, hugging himself. 'I love it!'

'If we're going to do it, then we'd better move fast,' Jack said. 'The Ice Children will be tumbling off their pedestals any minute now.'

'Well, you could always, you know . . .' Quilo held

up his hands and spread his fingers.

'Yes. Fine.' Jack sighed.

'I love it when this happens.' Quilo grinned at Bianca.

Jack threw a hand down, snowflake fingers spreading, ice shooting out in layers, building a bobsled with five seats. 'Get in, everyone.' Frost turned to Ishild. 'Sister, you must stay in your sleigh until the Ice Children call you. The city is cold enough for you to come, but you will need the power of their imaginations to settle and stay.'

Bianca turned to Pordis, looking for one last time into her spirit animal's chestnut eyes. A lump formed in her throat. She touched her forehead to the reindeer's, wrapping her arms round her neck and inhaling the musky smell of her coat. 'I love you, Pordis.'

'You are my herd, Bianca.'

Quilo jumped into the back seat of the bobsled. Jack climbed into the front.

'Come, Bianca!' Jack called.

As she tore herself away from Pordis, Bianca felt as if her heart were breaking.

'Where to?' asked Jack.

'The rose garden,' Bianca replied, trying to focus on the task ahead.

Bringing his snowflake hands together, Jack shot a flat stream of ice in front of them. Quilo looked back over his shoulder and, with a puff, propelled them forward. He let out a joyous *WHOOP!* as the sled rocketed along the track towards the coast, then shot down over the sea and up into the flashing colours of the Northern Lights.

Three minutes before midnight, on the longest night of winter, four days before Christmas, a shocking sound shook the city park. The jagged spit, pop and crackle of splintering ice split the air, accompanied by the lowing groans of glacial movement and the thundering of falling masses, as 209 icy pedestals shattered.

There came a clamour of amazed and hopeful adult voices as children stirred, and ice fell away from their bodies like flakes of salt.

Grown-ups rushed to help their frozen children and so none of them saw the bobsled made of ice shoot through the clouds above the park, descending like a rocket and skidding to a halt outside the rose garden.

Bianca scrambled out of the sled, stumbling over her feet in her hurry to see what was happening. Through the gap in the hedge, she saw her mum on her knees in a pool of ice shards, weeping for joy, embracing a confused-looking Finn, who was wrapped in a thick blanket.

'Bianca!' Her dad ran across the rose garden and

caught her up in his arms, hugging her to him. 'Oh, Bianca! You're here. Finn's here . . .' She was surprised to see his face crumple and his voice stall. 'I . . . I . . .'

'Don't cry, Dad,' she told him, hugging him hard. 'It's going to be OK.'

'Yanka,' Finn cried, and Bianca felt the bubble of emotion she'd been wrestling with since she'd first seen him frozen, pop. Tears ran down her cheeks as her brother struggled to his feet and ran to her. She picked him up and spun him around, revelling in his laughter. 'Mummy doesn't believe me, that I've been playing with the Snow Queen. Tell her it's true!'

'Oh yes, it's true all right. I saw you ride in her sleigh,' Bianca cried, kissing his cheeks.

'*Blearukkk!*' Finn complained.

'You're a kissing monster.'

Bianca's dad wrapped his arms round them all in a giant family hug.

Hearing a polite cough, Bianca turned to where Jack, Quilo, Pitter and Patter were waiting. She saw the look of surprise on her parents' faces at the sight of the little grey twins, the boy in the bear suit and the porcelain-white figure wearing a top hat.

'Finn, do you remember the promise we made Ishild?' Bianca asked her little brother.

'Yes.' Finn suddenly looked serious.

'We must keep it. We must start helping her right this very second.'

'Yes,' Finn agreed.

'Dad, Mum, these are our friends, Jack, Quilo, Pitter and Patter,' Bianca said. 'They helped me bring all of the children back, but now we need you to come with us. We have something very important to do.'

'But we should take Finn home.' Her mum shook her head. 'He needs to be warmed through. He hasn't eaten in weeks.'

'No! Finn protested, wriggling out of his blanket and his mum's arms. 'I'm not hungry.'

He took hold of Bianca's hand and she felt a surge of strength. 'You must listen to us, Mum, Dad. It's the winter solstice. Tonight is our chance to change the future of the world. We're going to do something incredible that will make everyone give their hearts to winter, and work to save it.'

Her parents looked bewildered, but they nodded.

Bianca turned to Quilo. 'Can you send up a whistling wind that will get everyone's attention?'

'That I can do.' Quilo looked delighted to have a job.

'Jack, can you write in the sky with your ice?'

'Write? What is "write"?'

'Human words.'

'I can't do that,' Jack admitted. 'But I can do frost feathers?'

'Dad, do you have a pen and paper?'

Bianca's dad rummaged in his coat pockets and pulled out a shopping list and a chewed biro.

Taking them from him, Bianca wrote some words, then handed the paper to Jack. 'Put these shapes in the sky and make them big so everyone can see them,' she said.

Quilo drew in the longest breath, then let out an ear-splitting whistle as Jack wrote the words in huge icy letters in the sky above the park.

ICE CHILDREN. COME. KEEP YOUR PROMISE.

28

WINTER SOLSTICE

The moon smiled down like a Cheshire cat, as excited children pulled their relieved and confused grown-ups towards the boating lake in the middle of the park. Soon the lakeside was lined with people.

Without being asked, the Ice Children, all 209 of them, stepped forward and joined hands. They remembered well the tears that had brought them home to their families and the promise they'd made to Ishild, the melting Snow Queen.

Closing their eyes, each child painted a picture of Winterton in their mind, remembering their feelings of joy and wonder at being there. As they did this, the boating lake at their feet transformed from a midnight liquid to a moonlit solid.

A woman screamed as two polar bears appeared from nowhere, skating out onto the ice on all fours before reaching out, clasping paws and pirouetting as a pair. The boating house had become an igloo, and a pair of puffins squawked, waving their wings excitedly at the ice skates on the shelf behind them.

'What is this?' Bianca's mum asked in amazement.

'Winter.' Bianca sighed happily, looking at all the reunited families around the lakeside.

There were gasps as the twinkling Flurry Flake appeared beyond the bandstand, and awed murmurs as the ground grew a blanket of thick snow. A hot-chocolate fountain materialized in the middle of the rose garden, and marshmallows bloomed on the bushes.

The Ice Children grabbed the hands of their grown-ups, gabbling excitedly that they'd really only been away for a day, and that they'd been playing in the wonderful Winterton.

Bianca smiled as she saw Casper take his dad's hand, leading him towards the rock garden, which had become a stony path that she knew would lead down to the sea, and the cove where Monodon would be waiting.

'*Bianca!*' came a voice inside her head, and she turned to see her Pordis standing there. She threw her arms round the reindeer, unable to prevent herself from sobbing. *'You mustn't cry, Bianca. I am always with you. You are my herd.'*

Hearing Finn laughing, Bianca looked up to see Sposh bouncing around her dad's feet. All around her, she heard cries of wonder and shrieks of delight.

A battalion of grown-ups was frantically making snowballs, suddenly as wild and carefree as their children. Bianca saw the doctor in his woollen coat shouting orders as he hurled the first snowball, and a new snow battle began. The polar bears on the frozen boating lake were giving skating classes to little ones, a unit of police officers was building a snowman and the helter-skelter had a queue of smiling people all drinking from their tin mugs, which brimmed with marshmallow-sprinkled hot chocolate.

Bianca heard the delicate chimes of sleigh bells.

'Look!' Sophie Lilley cried, and everyone turned their eyes skywards. Fat, puffy flakes of snow drifted down to kiss their cheeks.

'A unicorn!' Mrs Dorcas, the librarian, shrieked with excitement, clenching her fists and turning purple, as if she were about to explode with joy.

A choir of amazed sighs accompanied the Snow Queen's sparkling sleigh as it descended through the clouds and landed beside the frozen lake. Two snow golems rose from a snowdrift, one attending to the unicorn, the other standing ready with its hand outstretched, ready to assist Ishild.

All the Ice Children knelt, and the grown-ups, after glancing around, did the same.

Ishild stepped out of her sleigh, Snow personified, powerful and unmelting, hovering above the ground, surveying the gathering of humans.

'Tonight is the longest night of the year,' Ishild said in a voice with many notes, like the song of a wind harp. 'Let us spend it celebrating winter like we have never celebrated before, so that people will tell stories of this night for centuries to come and the memory will live long in your hearts!'

There was a high trill from the bandstand, and Bianca saw the Arctic orchestra was ready to play. The Arctic fox lifted her silver flute and the snowy owl began pecking away at the string of icicles hanging from the bandstand roof. The musk ox hummed a bass note and the walrus slapped at his blubbery belly.

Jack slid across the ice, reaching out a hand to Ishild. Whirling each other in silver-dusted arms, Snow and Frost flew across the lake, dancing a tango. They turned their heads, kicked up their legs and spun away from each other in a breathtaking routine. Pitter and Patter's feet rose and fell, landing slowly at first, building to a furious rhythm to accompany the dancers, their heads bobbing as they jigged along the shore. Standing beside the unicorn, Quilo jiggled his shoulders, and popped his bottom from side to side, in a time signature all of his own making.

'Come on, Yanka,' Finn cried, grabbing Bianca's hand and dragging her onto the ice to join in the merriment. She laughed as he bent his knees and threw his hands in the air as if he were trying to shake off a nest of biting ants. A heartbeat later, their dad and mum were there too, spinning around them, gasping and laughing as their children wriggled their shoulders and pulled faces to the undulating tunes of the Arctic animal orchestra. The Ice Children and their families danced the night away with the Frost, the Hail, the Sleet, the North Wind and the Snow, and it went down in the history books as the wildest winter party the city had ever seen.

29

CRYSTAL CREATURES

As the rosy light of dawn began to make the snow-swept city blush, the Snow Queen climbed back into her sleigh. The unicorn, who'd been giving children rides around the city park all night, returned to its harness. The Ice Children waved their goodbyes, repeating their promise to make the planet a place in which winter would always be welcome. Winterton, with its rides, games and winter creatures, began to fade.

Jack, Quilo, Pitter and Patter gathered with Bianca, Finn and the other Ice Children in the rose garden, where it had all started on the first of December.

'Will we ever see you again?' Finn asked mournfully, his eyes on the sky, even though Ishild had disappeared from view.

'What kind of a fool have we here?' asked Pitter.

'Why, you'll see us every year!' replied Patter.

'We will keep our promise, Jack,' Bianca said, and the Ice Children echoed her with a ripple of agreement and nodding heads.

'You once told me that love was the most powerful thing in the world,' Jack said to Bianca. 'Well, we got a lot of people to fall in love with winter this night.' Jack winked at her. 'Don't you think?'

'Yes,' Bianca said, smiling. 'And every year, on the longest night of winter, we will celebrate all that is wonderful about you and your season.'

'We all want to play in Winterton again,' Finn said.

'We don't want a world too warm for ice and snow,' Bianca said.

'No.' Finn shook his head. 'Never, ever, ever.'

'Oh, but I bet they don't mind seeing the back of hail and sleet . . .' grumbled Pitter, rolling his grey eyes.

'. . . cos of the irritating noise you make with those tapping feet.' Patter shoved him.

'Next time you visit the city, I'll go outside and dance,' Casper told them. 'I don't mind you pelting me with your hailstones.'

'Much obliged.' Pitter bowed his head.

'Bet he stays inside,' Patter whispered to Quilo.

'I think I want to be a vegetarian, to help the planet,' Gwen announced to her parents. 'I don't want to eat meat if it hurts Grendel.'

'Eating less meat will certainly help.' Quilo nodded approvingly. 'Those cow farts really heat up the atmosphere, I can tell you.' He waved his hand in front of his face. 'And they smell terrible! Phew!'

Bianca laughed, but then Jack caught her eye. 'What's wrong?'

'It's time for us to leave.'

'Oh!' Bianca didn't know when it had happened, but she'd grown fond of Frost. 'If you ever need me, you can leave a message on my window. And . . . thank you, for giving us a chance . . . and not taking our hearts.'

'Well . . .' Jack arched a white eyebrow. 'There's always next year.'

Stepping back onto the grass, top hat at a jaunty angle, Jack stood tall, right on the spot where Finn had first been found frozen. Pitter and Patter joined on either side, folding their arms and each lifting a foot as if they were about to dance. Quilo bounded over on all fours, the hood of his bear suit falling back to reveal his chubby cheeks. Jack placed his snowflake hands onto the shoulders of Pitter and Patter, and with a shimmer of silver and the sound of crumpling foil the four of them became figures of ice, rising up on a rectangular pedestal until they stood taller by far than all the children around them. There was a thunderous sound that shook the earth under their feet, and the ice took on the colour of granite, leaving only Jack's eyes entirely white.

Engraved in capital letters beneath the four figures were the words:

THERE ONCE WAS A TIME OF HARMONY

And it's up to us to bring it back, Bianca thought.

There was a long moment of silence, then the children and their grown-ups began drifting home. The sun chased away the darkness, lighting up the city's houses, snuggled under their blanket of snow.

'Where did you get that necklace?' Bianca's dad asked her. 'It's very pretty.'

Bianca put her hand to her neck and found a delicate silver chain there. Hanging from it was a crystal reindeer. 'Pordis!' She hugged the necklace to her chest.

'*My Bianca*,' came the warm voice inside her head. '*I will be with you, always.*'

'Sposh!' Finn exclaimed in delight, finding a crystal snow hare hanging round his own neck.

'I think it's time we all went home, don't you?' Bianca's mum said, hugging her two children to her.

And the Albedo family stumbled wearily, but happily, out of the park.

THERE ONCE
WAS A TIME
OF HARMONY

30

THE ICE CHILDREN

Every December since, on the longest night of the year, a winter festival has been held in the park.

It has become an annual tradition for Bianca and Finn to visit the rose garden at midnight and stand before the statue of Jack, Quilo, Pitter and Patter.

'Do you think they'll come this year?' Finn asked, tucking his red scarf into the neck of his coat.

'*We're* here, aren't we?' Bianca replied, smiling up at her brother. He was taller than she was now.

They heard a familiar fizz, a crackle and a creak like the opening of an old door, and watched as the whites of Jack Frost's eyes seemed to spread, infusing the granite sculpture with the properties of ice. Accompanied by a whip-crack snap, Jack stepped down from the pedestal. Quilo tumbled down after him, dressed as a bear as always, followed by the skittering Pitter and Patter.

'You've got older and bigger!' Quilo exclaimed.

'You're the same as ever,' Bianca said warmly.

'How is the Arctic?' Finn asked.

'The ice is still disappearing frighteningly fast,' Jack said, looking mournful.

'There are lots more of us now,' Bianca reassured him. 'Children all over the world are coming together, uniting to change things.'

'Lots of people feel the same way we do.' Finn nodded. 'We don't want the planet getting any warmer.'

'And things are changing,' Bianca said. 'In the summer, the city council voted to stop burning all fossil fuels, and they've just finished building a big wind farm off the coast, in the sea.'

'Oh yes! I like them!' Quilo boomed. 'It's fun blowing those windmill sails around.'

'We're grateful you do,' Bianca said. 'It makes energy to heat and light our homes.'

'Many of our vehicles are powered by the sun now,' Finn said. 'They don't belch carbon into the sky any more.'

Quilo burped, and Pitter and Patter giggled.

'The Ice Children are going out into the world and keeping their promise,' Bianca told them proudly.

'We all keep winter in our hearts,' Finn said, putting a hand over his own.

'Casper is on a ship measuring ice floes in the North Sea,' Bianca told them. 'He wrote to tell me that he's finally seen a narwhal. And Sophie Lilley is in the mountains of France, still with skis on her feet, learning ways to keep the snow from melting.'

'Gwen is the youngest-ever candidate for mayor,' Finn said. 'All her campaign promises are about preventing climate change. Her first act, if she gets elected, will be to change the name of the city to Winterton, to show the world how committed we are to preventing global warming.'

'Catchy name,' Quilo said.

'Is that original? I'm not sure . . .' asked Pitter.

'I think I've heard it somewhere before,' giggled Patter.

'We've learned that it's not enough for people to want change. Gwen says that it's governments that make laws and tax businesses, and that we need to become the government,' Bianca told them.

'Yes, and we're old enough to vote now.' Finn nodded. 'We can choose change and a way forward that will stop the Earth's temperatures rising.'

'We use our words and voices to protest the old industrial ways.' Bianca's hand went to the silver chain round her neck, and she caressed the crystal reindeer that hung there.

'I go to university next year,' Finn said proudly. 'I'm going to become a climate scientist.'

'What about you?' Jack asked Bianca. 'What are you doing?'

'Well . . .' Bianca found herself blushing. 'I write. I've been making my own silver book, all about a city where children are being frozen in ice.'

'I think I know that story,' Quilo quipped. 'Doesn't it have a devilishly handsome boy in a bear suit in it?'

'Yes, and he has a flatulence problem . . .' Patter said.

'. . . farts so powerful you can't stop 'em.' Pitter grinned.

'I'm hoping it will end up on shelves in homes and libraries all over the world. And when children hear the story, or read it, maybe they will be inspired to think about the little changes they can make in their daily lives to become one of the Ice Children. That way we will always have a winter.'

Jack smiled. 'I like that.'

'Mum is buying Downy Falls,' Finn told them.

'She's going to get a new printing press and fix

up the factory,' Bianca said, becoming excited. 'She wants to make beautiful books that celebrate nature.' She gave Jack a pointed look. 'Without using mirror shards!'

Laughing, Jack clapped. 'Wonderful. Now, who thinks we should invite my sister to our little gathering and decorate the city with snow?'

'Ishild!' Finn said breathlessly, looking up.

And, as if in reply, fat, fluffy flakes of snow fell from the sky, just like they always did on the longest night of winter.

ACKNOWLEDGEMENTS

We measure out our lives in seasons. We use them to describe our moods. We anticipate and memorialize them, associate them with colours and feelings, write songs and poetry about them. I cannot help but wonder what will happen to all this beautiful culture as temperatures rise. What will it mean to describe someone as having a wintry heart, if winters are warm and wet?

This story draws on the works of Hans Christian Anderson's *The Snow Queen*, Oscar Wilde's *The Selfish Giant* and *Pinocchio* by Carlo Collodi, flipping traditional motifs of winter being forbidding, frightening and heartless. In *The Ice Children* I have used the tropes of a fairy tale to respond to children's anxieties about climate change and global warming. Fairy tales were told to entertain but also warn young listeners about the dangers of the world. I want a world that has polar ice caps, glaciers and snow. I am one of the Ice Children. I wrote this story as a rallying cry for positive change.

This book is dedicated to my agent Kirsty McLachlan,

whom I respect, admire and am enormously grateful to have on my side. *The Ice Children* production on Audible and this beautiful book wouldn't exist if it wasn't for her. She fought for it, and me, and I will never forget that. Thank you, Kirsty. I will always be in your debt.

This is the story that almost broke me. It's thanks to my husband and manager, Sam Harmsworth-Sparling, and my best friend, Claire Rakich, that it didn't. It was written in extraordinary times. Their endless cheerleading and cups of tea kept me going. Thank you.

I am tremendously grateful to every member of the team at Macmillan for creating this book, in particular Rachel Vale for the incredible design, Sarah Plows and Jo Hardacre for telling the world about it, Samantha Smith for believing in my stories. This story is a true collaboration. It's been through more editors than any other story I've written and they've all helped shape it. Thanks to: Imogen Papworth from Audible, Lucy Rogers, Venetia Gosling, Nick de Somogyi, but especially my legendary Macmillan editor and friend Sarah Hughes who has faced Herculean trials whilst shepherding this story and yet has guided it into bookshops like a flipping boss. Thank you, Sarah. I hope you know how much I love working with you.

I wanted this book to be beautiful and full of winter magic. And it's as if the artist Penny Neville-Lee looked into my imagination, waved her wand and granted my wish. She is responsible for the extraordinary cover and all the wonderful internal illustrations you see. Thank you, Penny. Your pictures and my words are a perfect pairing.

Years ago, when I was writing my beetle books, I visited a good friend. I was sitting in the passenger seat of her car, telling her the beginning of this story as it had come to me, of Finn being found frozen in the park. Her three young children, who were sitting in the back, fell silent. She turned to me and said, 'You have to write it – look.' She nodded back at her children. 'They're listening. They want to know what happens next.' She was right. Thank you, Karen Minto, Dylan, Seren and Evan. I hope you approve of the way this story has turned out.

And, in case you are wondering, my winter spirit animal is an Arctic Wolf. What's yours?

ABOUT THE AUTHOR

M. G. Leonard has made up stories since she was a girl, but back then adults called them lies or tall tales and she didn't write them down. As a grown-up, her favourite things to create stories about are beetles, birds and trains. Her books have been translated into over forty languages and have won many awards. She is the vice-president of the insect charity Buglife, and a founding author of Authors4Oceans. She lives in England, by the sea, with her husband, two sons, a dog called Nell and a variety of exotic beetles.

ABOUT THE ILLUSTRATOR

Penny Neville-Lee was raised on a healthy diet of Saturday cartoons and MGM musicals. Never happier than when creating, she spent her early years drawing and making and was rarely found without a doodle somewhere in the margins. Penny studied MA Painting at the Royal College of Art. She is inspired by small people, bright colours, a blank page and newly sharpened pencils. She lives in Manchester with her two children, her husband and a very adventurous cat.